JERUSALEM
MOSAIC

JERUSALEM

MOSAIC

YOUNG
VOICES
FROM THE
HOLY CITY

I. E. Mozeson &
Lois Stavsky

Four Winds Press
New York

Maxwell Macmillan Canada
Toronto

Maxwell Macmillan International
New York Oxford Singapore Sydney

Special thanks to photographer Leora Cheshin for the photographs on pages 13, 57, 85, and 123. These photographs were taken in Jerusalem during the summer of 1993.

Four Winds Press
Macmillan Publishing Company
866 Third Avenue
New York, NY 10022

Maxwell Macmillan Canada, Inc.
1200 Eglinton Avenue East, Suite 200
Don Mills, Ontario M3C 3N1

Macmillan Publishing Company is part of the
Maxwell Communication Group of Companies.

First edition
Printed and bound in the United States of America

10 9 8 7 6 5 4 3 2 1

The text of this book is set in Calligraphic
Book design by Andrea Schneeman

Library of Congress Cataloging-in-Publication Data
Mozeson, Isaac.
    Jerusalem mosaic : young voices from the Holy City / I.E. Mozeson
and Lois Stavsky. — 1st ed.
        p.   cm.
    Includes bibliographical references and index.
    ISBN 0-02-767651-X
    1. Jewish teenagers—Jerusalem—Interviews—Juvenile literature.
2. Teenagers, Palestinian Arab—Jerusalem—Interviews—Juvenile
literature.   3. Jewish-Arab relations—Juvenile literature.
4. Jerusalem—Ethnic relations—Juvenile literature.   5. Jerusalem-
-Social Conditions—Juvenile literature.   6. Jerusalem—Social
conditions.   [1. Jerusalem—Ethnic relations.   2. Youth—Jerusalem-
-Interviews.   3. Jewish-Arab relations.]   I. Stavsky, Lois.
II. Title.
DS109.85M68   1994
305.23'5'089924056.9442—dc20   94-21439
                                                          CIP   AC

To peace for the City of Peace:

Pray for the peace of Jerusalem. . . . Peace be within thy walls
                              —the Hebrew Bible

Blessed are the peacemakers: for they shall be called the children of God
                              —the New Testament

If the enemy inclines toward peace, do thou also incline toward peace
                              —the Koran

To peace for the City of Peace:

Pray for the peace of Jerusalem. . . . Peace be within thy walls
                                                     —the Hebrew Bible

Blessed are the peacemakers: for they shall be called the children of God
                                                     —the New Testament

If the enemy inclines toward peace, do thou also incline toward peace
                                                     —the Koran

CONTENTS

A mosaic is

a work of art made by arranging different-colored stones. In the ancient language of the Bible, the words for "children," "stones," and "building" share a common root. A wall, a city, and a nation must be built one layer of stone, one generation, at a time. According to municipal law, every wall and building in the Holy City must be built of Jerusalem stone. Somehow, each stone in this uniquely beautiful and compelling city is as different as her children.

This book presents the various textures of ancient Jerusalem's modern mosaic. By listening to the youth of Jerusalem, through their own words, we can share the present and imagine the future of a city with the most toppled and rebuilt walls in human history.

Explore this collection of stones and you find young representatives of many nationalities, ethnic groups, and religious and political views. The summers of 1992 and 1993 provided a particularly exciting time to examine and record the newest layer of Jerusalem stone. The Gulf War was just far back enough to discuss with calm, the Israeli elections produced a major political shift, and large waves of Jewish immigrants from the former Soviet Union and Ethiopia had just settled in. The Arab *intifada*, or uprising against Israeli rule, was winding down, while peace talks promised a new era of self-rule and ethnic pride for the city's Moslem and Christian minorities. The breakthrough Israeli-PLO agreement of fall 1993 produced both new fears and new hopes about ancient enemies learning to live side by side.

News stories about expelled Moslem radicals, clashes between secular and ultrareligious Israelis, and the high unemployment rate were also sounded out among these young people of Jerusalem, ages twelve through twenty. Although our interviews began with neutral topics like family history and school and social life, many of the teenagers were reluctant to use their real names or to be recorded on tape or photographed. Ultrareligious Jewish youth were our most reluctant subjects. For them, talking to people outside of their community is often seen as immodest or potentially threatening.

The edited monologues are the result of interviews with teens whom we largely met at random, in their neighborhoods, on the main pedestrian mall, and at the few parks where Arab and Jewish youth cross paths. While it was tougher to find and conduct our interviews this way, we found fresh, candid voices rather than the usual spokespersons made available to journalists.

All but a few of these interviews were conducted in Hebrew or English. As these were some of our subjects' second languages, we are grateful that so many Arab, Armenian, Ethiopian, and Russian youngsters put in the extra effort to understand and make themselves understood. We explained to them that readers all over the world care about their opinions and how they view their lives in this incomparable city. Like all Jerusalemites, these young people are living on the edge — because everywhere in Jerusalem one lives on the border of someone else's world. Walk the streets of Jerusalem and you come across people whose world and vision were formed in nineteenth-century Armenia, seventeenth-century Poland, seventh-century Arabia, first-century Ethiopia, and twentieth-century America. There are so many intersecting time zones that Jerusalem can only be described as timeless space.

In the Bible, Jerusalem first appears in the book of Joshua — but believers fit the Holy City into a crucial early moment in biblical history. In Gen. 22 the Bible records Abraham's binding of his son Isaac and his readiness to sacrifice him according to God's will. According to tradition, this took place on Jerusalem's Mount Zion, the future site of the Holy Temple. Christianity makes this event special by seeing it as a prophetic foreshadowing of God's son, Jesus, whose life would be sacrificed to give mankind salvation from sin. In Moslem lore it was Abraham's firstborn son, Ishmael, ancestor of the Arab people, who was bound to the altar by Ilbrahim (Abraham).

In this first moment of Jerusalem's history we already have three major faiths with different, even competing visions. In the long history of Jerusalem we see that, tragically, this holiest of cities has been the stage for many replays of the Cain and Abel act of Gen. 4 — murdering one's brother in spiritual competition.

Look at a map and see how the tiny land of Israel (about the size of New Jersey) has huge significance as the crossroads of three continents. Ancient Christian maps of the world put Jerusalem at the center of three circles representing Europe, Asia, and Africa. Such a well-situated place is perfect for influencing and being influenced in the world's marketplace of ideas. Then again, any imperial army wishing to march from Alexandria, Egypt, to Damascus, Syria, has to control the eastern Mediterranean and its fortress capital of Jerusalem in the Judean hills. The brief history that follows shows how Jerusalem has been both a political and a spiritual prize down through the centuries.

■ ß ■
■

Abed
(age 19)

My parents and I were born in Silwan. This is the Arab village just outside the Old City walls. We are very close to Al-Aksa Mosque and the Jewish Quarter. I don't have a street address. It would be crazy to name all the winding alleyways of Silwan. Anyone can find us by asking for my uncle's grocery store. Any mail for us also comes to this store.

Our house has two rooms. I have four brothers and six sisters.

The youngest is five. Since my father died in 1990, I have been like the father of the family. Things are very hard these days, but, *inshallah* [with Allah's help], I find work every once in a while.

Life was much better in the time of my grandparents. I often listen to the old men talking over their coffee and smoking pipes. Under the Turks and the British, we lived here outside the city walls with many Yemenite Jews. These were sweet, religious people who spoke Arabic and worked in simple crafts. They were always respectful and shy. My grandfather would get on his donkey early each morning to deliver milk to many Jewish families. He was always invited into their homes. There were many close friendships between Jews and Arabs. My grandmother told us how she nursed a Jewish baby when its mother died.

Boys would have plenty of work drawing water from the Shiloh spring. Now the Israelis have pipes of water going to every house. The spring water is much better. You have to taste it to see how sweet it is. And bathing in this water will heal you of many afflictions.

I went to school on Mount Scopus from age six to sixteen. I then went to school in Abu Tor. This was a state school not run by the Wakif, the Moslem religious authority. This is where my good English is coming from. We had Jewish and Christian teachers there. I liked this school, but I had to leave after my father died. It was my responsibility to bring home more money. No one else in my family is earning money, but my oldest sister is studying to be a teacher. It is easier for girls to stay in school. They don't have to support the family.

It is not easy to live on Israeli shekels. The Jordanian dinar was much better. It brought more food into the house. My father used to clean and plaster houses. I am prepared to do this, too, but I enjoy working in hotels and supermarkets. Now there are Russians working in these places. In the hotel across the park I work four hours a day for five hundred shekels a month. The Russians get eight hours of work a day, and they earn two thousand shekels a month. They get two times what I earn. I am in this park too many afternoons without work after the morning has passed. I know that no one will give me work here, but at least people from my village will not see me here. I should be waiting at the city gates to be picked for work, but this is only donkeywork.

Our relatives in Gebel Mukhbar cannot help us. I have one relative in New Jersey, America, who helps a little. I often write to them and send pictures. This is also like a job. Last year I had stones thrown at me for trying to leave Silwan to find work. It was a strike day, so I was punished for breaking the strike. I don't support the strikes, because they only make things harder. In the villages these strikes don't hurt people. They get money from the PLO [Palestine Liberation Organization] or from Jordan. And they have land. They can live from their own vegetables and fruits and animals. In Silwan we no longer have land near our homes. We used to be a village of five thousand. Now we are fifty thousand. People came to find work in Jerusalem. But now, without land, if we don't work, we don't eat.

I do not support the politics of the PLO or Hamas. I voted for Labor. I didn't worry about Rabin's strong words during the *intifada*, the Arab uprising. First he said to break our bones; now he says nice things. These are only words. Prime Minister Rabin is a politician. But maybe the new party in power will make things better. We always voted for Teddy Kollek in city elections.

I would like to see Jerusalem be international. Let all nations have a part in her, and not any one country. I don't know what to do with the other problems of peace. Perhaps when there is autonomy in the territories, there will be no more struggles and killing. We only lost one relative to wars. That was in 1967. In the Persian Gulf War I saw scud missiles from a rooftop where I was staying illegally on a job. I didn't wear a gas mask. Why should I worry about getting killed? Everything is up to Allah.

Right now, I don't pray five times a day like I used to. But I am still religious inside. There are too many crazy extremists here, Jewish and Arab. We don't have pictures of venerated leaders in our house. Not of Saddam, not of Arafat, not of King Hussein. We are plain people.

I would like to get married, but it cannot be so soon. I must make more than five hundred shekels a month. It is not our way to talk to girls directly. When I am ready to marry, I will speak to a girl's parents. They will check to see if I am trustworthy. After a few days I would get an answer. I could marry a non-Arab girl without problems from my family. She would not have to convert to Islam. But, yes, the children would have to be brought up as Moslems. In Silwan there are at least fifty Jewish girls who are married to Moslems. Also, Christian girls who marry Moslems are more accepted here than inside the Old City walls. They are all loved by everyone in our village.

Tourists and Jews do not come to Silwan. But it is not a bad place like some people say. There is more concern in Silwan for where you work than where you worship. I prefer to be in hotels in West Jerusalem than in the Moslem Quarter, where so many people know my family.

If I had the money to work in Paris or New York, I would do it. After a few years of sending money home, I would come back myself. Everything will be possible if there will be peace. This will be best for us and all the children.

Alon
(age 15)

My mother was born in South Africa, and my father in America. They met here in Israel. As youngsters they were both active in Habonim, a Zionist youth movement. I suppose that is why they decided to move here to Israel. My father works now as a lawyer and my mother as an artist.

I've lived in Jerusalem all my life, in a nine-room house in German Colony. In the past few years I've seen many positive changes. My neighborhood borders on Katamon, and I used to be disturbed by the crudeness of some of my Moroccan neighbors. I hate it when people yell things like "son of a dog" at each other. But the people here are becoming better mannered. There is certainly less coarseness among the newer immigrants. And people, in general, are less likely to push ahead of you on buses these days.

I've even begun to see more of a concern for the environment. Israel is still way behind most Western countries that I've visited, but it is now possible to buy recycled paper and other goods. Israelis are definitely becoming less wasteful.

And, of course, I'm thrilled by the election results. For the first time in my life, Labor is back in power. I think now there may be some movement toward equality of Arabs and Jews. I don't know if there can ever be peace in this region, but I think the Palestinians deserve far better treatment than they had been getting under Likud.

It really disturbs me to see pictures of people living in refugee camps. I think these regions should be given autonomy, and the Palestinians should be allowed to rebuild their lives. I don't blame these Palestinians for hating Jews. If I were given army service in a refugee camp in Gaza, I would refuse to serve. I'd rather sit in jail.

Yet I'm not willing to give the Palestinians all the land we captured from them in 1967. Jerusalem must always remain in Jewish hands. I haven't yet made up my mind about West Bank towns like Hebron. But it is time for the Israeli army to withdraw from land settled by Palestinians. At some time in the not-too-distant future there will be a Palestinian state, whether we want it or not. It is, therefore, to Israel's advantage to have as much input as possible in the establishment of such a state.

Unfortunately, I don't see any permanent peace in this

region. I think that the Arabs and the Jews are both going to continue to claim the land here. And I don't think that the establishment of a Palestinian state can rid this region of hatred. The hate and distrust are too deep on both sides. I've never really had an Arab friend and I've never visited the Moslem Quarter of Jerusalem. I'm afraid of the hatred that my presence would provoke. And this is why there will always be an Israeli army.

Army service is part of life here. My sister is now in the army and she generally has few complaints. But she did complain when she was locked in a small shed for a whole day with her troop because a few of the girls were smoking and fooling around. But I think collective punishment is necessary. Surrounded by enemies, we Jews in Israel must have unity. Despite any grievances I've had with some of its policies, I am looking forward to serving this country.

I have a good life here. My school day begins at seven and sometimes ends as early as ten. My longest day is over at one. After school I come home and eat, sleep, and listen to music. I especially like heavy metal. My favorite groups are Metallica and Guns n' Roses. I have all their hits on discs.

Sometimes I get together with friends. I used to belong to the Scouts, but I never liked it. It was a pain in the butt, so I dropped out. I'm not bored when I'm alone. I keep busy. So do most of the kids I know. I've never known any of my classmates to be involved with drugs, or crime, or casual sex. Soon I will have to start studying for the *bagrut*, the national exams for high school graduates. After army service I would like to go to the Hebrew University.

I would want to raise my family right here in Jerusalem. There is something special about this place, something holy. I, myself, don't believe in God, although I do think that there is something spiritual beyond us. But I don't believe in the kind of God that could have allowed the Holocaust to happen. It doesn't make sense to me. The topic of religion never comes up at home.

Occasionally we attend a reform service on Shmuel HaNagid Street. Once I asked my father if he believes in God. He told me, "Vaguely." I've never discussed religion with my mother. She lights candles Friday night and the whole family eats together. Sometimes my father even makes *kiddush*. The Sabbath is a special time of the week for us and a tradition that I would like to continue. But my parents don't fast on Yom Kippur [the Day of Atonement], and neither will I. Even though I am not religious, I like the special feeling of Shabbat [the Sabbath day, Saturday] in Jerusalem. I really would not like to see buses running before evening on Shabbat. I more or less like the status quo. I don't like, though, when people try to change me. Just yesterday a couple of guys in town asked me if I wanted to put on *tefillin* [ritual prayer straps]. I simply said, "No thanks," and walked away. If someone tried to force me, I'd probably punch him in the nose.

I wish Israel were cleaner, like Switzerland, and had strict recycling laws, like Germany. Someday that will come. In the meantime, there is nowhere else I'd rather live.

Ani
(age 20)

I feel like a bird in a cage. Every night at ten o'clock the Armenian convent, our whole section, is locked up for the night. No outsiders are allowed in after ten. We need a good reason for coming in or out after curfew. There is no longer any danger that keeps the high walls around the convent so cut off from the world. But our quarter had to be secured against persecution for so many centuries that I guess it is a tradition now.

I was born here in the convent and went to school across the street at the Rosary Sisters School. We learned much about the Armenian Orthodox rite, but the school is not only for religious studies. Biology was my best subject in school. My dream is to study nutrition in an American college. I know older people who almost never leave the Old City, but I love getting out whenever I can. The money is a problem now, so I might have to go to a college here in Jerusalem.

My parents were born and were married here. The only grandparent I know is my mother's mother. She was born in Sasson, near Armenia. My mother's side is spread out all over. I have relatives in Jordan, Lebanon, Armenia, the United States, and here in Jaffa and Haifa. This is not unusual for an Armenian family. My father's side includes many Christian Arabs. My father died when he was quite young. He was working in Libya at the time. We were told that he died of a heart attack. We will never know if this is really the truth. Our relatives have helped us out ever since. My mother has also remained very strong. She still works in an old-age home in West Jerusalem and in a gold factory in the Christian Quarter.

Whenever I travel, it is always to visit relatives. My best trip was in 1990 when I went to my uncle's home in Pasadena, California. There is a good-size Armenian community there. But I must admit I really liked San Francisco and San Diego much better. It would be my dream to live in one of those cities. I visit other cousins a few times a year in Jordan, Jaffa, and Haifa. I can no longer visit relatives in Lebanon because of the troubles there. The Syrians make life difficult for the Christians there, and nobody seems to care. We still have Jordanian passports so it is easy for us to get over the Allenby Bridge to Jordan. I am always glad to return to Israel, though, even in my little "birdcage."

Both the Israelis and the Jordanians respect us. We never get into trouble or make demands. Throughout the *intifada* we stayed neutral. When the gangs threw rocks and bottles in the other quarters, our teenage boys knew to come right home. Occasionally we have had to run out of our homes when clouds of tear gas blew our way. Some of us have stores in the Christian and Moslem quarters. We had to close them during PLO strikes. When my brother-in-law's jewelry factory stayed open, he received threats that his place would get blown up. We were allowed to keep our schools open, which was fortunate for me. We did not support or condemn the *intifada*. I have some sympathies for people without a homeland. But why should we get involved? Did anyone help the Armenians during the Turkish genocide? Who is helping us now?

Anyway, I hope the *intifada* is over. The climate is better for peace now with the change in government. Very few Armenians voted in the Israeli elections and we don't serve in the army. There are good things about army service, but we can't consider it. It would be taking sides.

It would be good if the Palestinians had their own state in the West Bank and Gaza. They should not have an army, though. Too many people would get killed, especially one group against the other. And there should be open borders between Israel and these Palestinian homelands. The Old City of Jerusalem could be run by the United Nations. There are places of worship here that represent at least thirty countries I can think of. It's already a united nations here.

The 1967 war was important to our community because so many of us were in Jordan. The scariest time I remember was the Persian Gulf War. We all went into sealed rooms and we wore masks for the first several alarms. We didn't know what Saddam would do. We didn't think he cared to avoid killing his own people here in Jerusalem or in Jaffa near Tel Aviv. It was a frightening time. No one wanted Israel to suffer damage from the missiles or to get into another war.

The Gulf War also hurt our business. But now the tourists are back and our store is doing better than ever. I am doing more of the painting and ceramics work now, and not just selling. I enjoy working with art, but this is a trap. It will keep me living here and not following my plans for college. I have no real chance of meeting an Armenian boyfriend here. Certainly not one that I meet on my own.

We are a small community of less than three hundred permanent residents. But we get visitors from all over the Armenian Diaspora. Because we don't have our own home- land in Armenia, this ancient religious and cultural center in Jerusalem is practically our capital. Of course, we have many non-Armenian tourists visiting us, too. It is fun to meet peo- ple from all over the world in my ceramics shop.

It is out of the question for someone in our community to marry a Moslem or Jew. Even a Roman Catholic husband would be an intermarriage for my family. I am not as reli- gious as my grandmother, but I certainly don't want to dis- appoint my whole family by marrying out of our faith.

I would like to meet my husband during another trip to California. Even if I lived in California, I would like to keep up with our holy days and customs. I would be very happy to live in the U.S. but I would come back here to visit. This is my little cage, but it is also my home.

Ariella
(age 12)

My parents met when they were high school students in Los Angeles. After they finished high school, they spent a year together in kibbutz. They were married a year later when they were nineteen.

It was my mother's dream to settle in Israel. Both her parents are Zionists. They had talked all their lives about making *aliyah* [immigrating to Israel]. They had managed to escape from Germany in time to avoid the camps. But almost no other family members survived. If my father hadn't met my mother, he might still be living in America. Both his parents are Holocaust survivors. My grandfather lost his first wife and daughter at Auschwitz. My father was raised as a secular Jew. His family still lives in Los Angeles. My mother's parents are now in the Rehavia neighborhood in central Jerusalem.

When I was six months old, my parents made *aliyah* to Tel Aviv. Two years later they moved to the Emek Refaim neighborhood, near the Natural Science Museum. I live in a nine-room villa. Just last year—after my brother was born—we added another room. The Arab builder became a close friend of our family. He visits us for dinner often. My parents now rent out the extra room to someone who helps my mother around the house.

My father enjoys his work. He works for the Ministry of Defense as a city planner for Tel Aviv. Unfortunately, he has to travel a lot. We've gotten used to it, but we miss him. Especially when he's gone for a month at a time. My mother used to work at the Israel Museum, but now she stays at home with us three kids.

My neighborhood has changed quite a bit in the past ten years. Emek Refaim used to be a fairly ordinary middle-class neighborhood with many Eastern European Jews. There were few stores. But in the past few years many Anglo-Saxim [immigrants from English-speaking countries] began to settle here. Now it is a fun place with lots of cafés, pizza shops, fancy hair salons and boutiques. I hear English everywhere. I really like living here. I think it is the best neighborhood in Jerusalem.

A few years ago the Anglo-Saxim in nearby Baka established an alternative religious school. And that's where I go to school. But it is nothing like it's supposed to be. I don't feel that I have been getting an education. The teachers in my so-called progressive school are not open to discussions. They never try anything new. They give us too many worksheets, and most of them don't seem to like getting involved with us students. There's too much emphasis on *limudei kodesh* [religious subjects]. We spend most of the time on Hebrew scripture and hardly any on history or humanities or the arts. I don't feel that I have a basic understanding of even Jewish history. I wish I could go to the Masorati [traditional conservative] school instead. But it doesn't accept too many students, so I have to do well enough to qualify for admission next year.

When I'm not in school, I like working on my art and going swimming. I'm only five minutes from the municipal pool on Emek Refaim Street. I also love horseback riding.

After army service I would like to go to college in the States to study architecture. Then I will return to Israel. Though I like spending time abroad, I would not want to live anywhere but here. We visit the States frequently, and I have many friends in Los Angeles and New York. None of them have the freedom that I have. Here in Jerusalem I can walk around at any time of day or night. I never feel unsafe. This country really is a paradise for children. Everyone treats us with respect. Also, what other city in the world has the beauty of Jerusalem?

Not that there aren't tensions here. My family isn't especially observant. We travel on Shabbat. I often feel that the religious kids in my school look down on me because we aren't more religious. Also, some of my teachers make me feel like I'm not as good as the more observant kids.

We never used to go to any synagogue, but now we do. There is a reform synagogue, Kol Neshamah, a few blocks from my home. The rabbi is an American from New York and he's friendly to everyone. Every Friday night we join about two hundred other people—mostly Americans—for services. I had my Bat Mitzvah in Kol Neshamah this year. I can't imagine going to a *bet knesset* where men and women have to sit apart.

I would like to see more women in positions of power in this country. They don't seem to have the same opportunities that men do, and too few of them are represented in the Knesset. I am glad that Shulamit Aloni is in the cabinet, and I am happy that Likud is out of power. Maybe now there can be some kind of peace. At least there's a chance with everything that the Labor party is arranging with the PLO.

I like the general idea of getting closer to our Arab enemies and figuring out ways that allow everyone to live in peace side by side. But I don't like Arafat himself. The world sees him as a "nice guy" who loves peace, rather than somebody who we are forced to deal with at this time. I doubt the honesty of any of those professional terrorists. I am hopeful that things will work out better with everyday Palestinian Arabs who want a better life but don't have dreams about making Israel disappear. I was happy about the agreements with the PLO, but Peres and Rabin should not have made the Gaza-Jericho deal into such a surprise.

I am not ready to give the Palestinians a state of their own, but I think they should be given autonomy within their own territories. We don't even know how they would manage their own affairs, or if they can. Their villages seem dirty, and that bothers me. Giving them control of Gaza and Jericho is a good beginning, but I don't see any real changes in attitudes coming soon.

I don't want to see any of our settlements taken apart. But I don't like the hard line that Likud and the other right-wing parties take. We have to be willing to at least talk about "land for peace." If the Palestinians are prepared to make sacrifices, then so should we.

Maybe the new government will spend less time arguing among themselves. If the politicians in this country could only agree, maybe something could be accomplished. I also feel that it's about time the *haredim* [ultra-orthodox Jews] started giving something to this country. They should not get the benefits of this state if they refuse to do army service. According to the Torah, if there is a war, one must fight. What right do they have to ask for money from a government they don't even support?

I am happy that so many new immigrants have come in the past few years. I wish, though, that the Russian kids weren't so cliquish. They don't even give us a chance to get to know them. There are quite a few in my school, and they only talk to each other.

I suppose that most of the new immigrants will want to stay in this country. Who wouldn't? Even if I were to fall in love and to marry someone abroad who wasn't Jewish, I'd want to return here to raise our family.

Avner
(age 18)

I was born
and raised in Beit
Hakerem, not far from the
Hadassah Hospital where I
am working. My parents are sabras
[native-born Israelis]; it is only my
grandparents who came here from
Poland and Russia. They came here
in the twenties. We in Beit Hakerem
are almost in a separate village
away from Jerusalem. The old
sections of our neighborhood have
changed very little since my grandparents' time. But Jerusalem is an-

other story. I am only eighteen and I can't believe the changes I have seen in my life.

Many of the new neighborhoods around the city center are filled with new immigrants. They are all welcome in my eyes. That is what this country is all about. I probably wouldn't date an Ethiopian girl myself, but I think that eventually there will be no differences between immigrant groups.

I have visited England and the United States. It is possible that I would take a job in another country for two years maximum. I would save money and bring it back here. For me there is no living anywhere but here.

I only missed voting in the elections because I was too young by five weeks. I would have voted for Labor, so you know I am happy with the results. I'm not for a socialist system, and Labor has moved away from such positions anyway. I do believe in "land for peace." I am not talking about a separate state for Palestinians. That is full of danger. I would hold on to the Golan and let most of or all of the West Bank be in confederation with Jordan. Gaza would be better as part of Egypt, as it was before.

I can't really complain about the educational system. A student who wants to can get a lot out of school. My school allowed me to have this job as a research assistant at Hadassah Hospital. I am learning a great deal from helping graduate students and doctors. Of course, I'll learn a lot in the army very soon. I don't like the fact that so many Arabs and religious Jews my age get out of army service.

The *haredim* are more afraid of secular influences in the army than of any physical dangers. They should serve just like the religious Zionists do in their *hesder yeshivot*. The *hesder yeshiva* students prove that you can learn Torah [Jewish law and lore] and learn to fight at the same time. Instead of being afraid of losing their faith while serving in the army, why don't they join so they can try to influence others? They have a right to their beliefs and a right to have political power. But I don't like it when religious parties get much more power than their numbers should allow. This is what happened in 1988. Sure there are some tensions between religious and secular, but why should life not have any tensions?

Very soon I will be serving in the Israeli army. I want very much to serve in a combat unit. This has nothing to do with politics. The army is part of your life.

In my other hospital duties I see Arab patients and Arab ambulance drivers. To me they are only people needing help. Almost all of them appreciate what our hospital does for them, so I don't see much hostility. I even helped set up beds for a wounded Arab terrorist and his Jewish victim. When the ambulance brought them both in, they were both side by side for a while, attached to similar IVs.

I have never myself been a victim of any terrorism or hostilities. The only war I remember was not really a war. Only before the first scud attack were some of us a little hysterical. We soon got used to it, and I didn't bother with gas masks after the fourth or fifth missile attack. The casualties were low in Tel Aviv because the houses were built well and the civil defense advice was so good. Israel did the right thing by staying out of the Persian Gulf War. If more of our people were getting killed, then we would have no choice.

Security is Israel's number one problem. If we could have peace, then all our resources could go into creating a healthy economy. Without the corruption of Likud, such money would make this country great.

Chaim
(age 13)

My family

made *aliyah* in 1983. I was four years old at the time. We were living on the Lower East Side of Manhattan, but I don't really remember much about our life in *galut* [exile]. My mother tells me that she always felt like a "guest" in America. Now she is home.

Most of my mother's family is now living in Israel. My father's family still lives on the Lower East Side. They were not happy when we made *aliyah*. They miss us and they worry about our safety. But my parents feel safer here than they ever felt in New York.

When we first came to Israel, we went directly to the Absorbtion Center in Mevaseret Zion. We thought we would be there for about a year, but we ended up spending two years there. My parents had bought an apartment in Pisgat Ze'ev, a new development in East Jerusalem. Because the area was still undeveloped, my parents were able to get a three-bedroom apartment with a backyard at a price they could afford. But it took longer than they had expected to be built.

Every few weeks we would drive by and see that a little bit more got built. When I first saw the floor, I said to myself, How will we ever be able to live in this house? When will it ever be ready? All the builders were Arabs. I thought of them as my friends, because they were building my new home.

At the time there was no road that bypassed the surrounding Arab villages. And on the way to Pisgat Ze'ev we always drove by Shuafat, the neighboring Arab village. I was impressed by the huge villas that our Arab neighbors live in. Now there are two roads that go directly from the center of town to Pisgat Ze'ev. If there weren't, there would be problems, because the Arabs in Shuafat often throw stones at cars with yellow [Israeli] license plates. Before the *intifada* I never heard of any problems with the Arabs in Shuafat. But all that has changed.

The most exciting thing that happened to us in the Absorbtion Center was the arrival of dozens of Ethiopian immigrants about a year after we arrived. Soon tourist buses and all kinds of important people were visiting Mevaseret Zion. Everybody was making a big fuss over the Ethiopians. I remember posing for a picture with an Ethiopian kid. We were giving flowers to New York mayor Ed Koch when he visited Mevaseret.

My family "adopted" an Ethiopian family with whom we are still in touch. I thought they were a little strange, especially their food. They were always eating this weird kind of bread. But I was happy to help them out. They were strangers, and I was already somewhat used to life here. A few years later my parents adopted an Ethiopian baby girl. My sister is now seven years old.

I am glad that my parents decided to move to this country. I would never want to live anywhere else. The atmosphere here is special. The sights are splendid. There is always something new to discover. Just this morning my father, my brother, and I climbed Masada. From the top of this ancient fortress high up on the mountain, we saw the sun rise above the Dead Sea. What a sight!

Another good thing about this country is that everyone treats everyone else like family. People are friendly. Especially the religious Jews. This past year I was learning in a settlement in Elon Moreh, near Shechem [Nablus]. People I didn't even know invited me to their homes.

This past year that I spent in Elon Moreh has changed my feelings toward Arabs. I couldn't ride anywhere without having rocks thrown at me by Arabs. I feel now that I hate them. I know that there are some good ones, but the bad ones are the majority.

The majority want us either dead or out of our country. I have no sympathy for them because they have about nine countries and we just have one. My teacher was a Kach supporter and would go into Arab villages with some friends to cause trouble. They would close up the streets. My teacher would shoot in the air to scare the Arabs. He felt that if Jewish cars couldn't move freely in Arab territory, then no cars should. I agree. But what he did is against the law. If he had been caught, he would have been arrested. My dorm counselor was once arrested for beating up an Arab who was yelling, "Death to the Jews."

When I'm on the city bus and the Arabs start throwing stones at us, my friends and I yell, "Death to the Arabs." It's not that we want the Arabs dead. It's just that we are afraid of their violence.

If I had my way, there would be no Arabs in this country. I don't feel that Jews should have to walk around armed in their own land, just a few meters from their own homes. We fought and died for every bit of this land. If the Arabs had a chance, they would butcher us like animals. Just today two Israeli soldiers were killed up north near the Jordanian border.

The results of the last elections frighten me. I am afraid that Rabin will be giving up more than Gaza and Jericho to the Arabs. Rabin's shaking hands with Arafat is like a mouse shaking hands with a cat. Arafat only wants to destroy us. He'll lie about peace and then attack us with all the new men and weapons he'll bring into Gaza and Jericho.

If I could have voted, I would have voted for Moledet. Not only wouldn't I give up even an inch of this land, but I would transfer any Arabs who got in the way. I think Rabin is in for some hard times if he thinks people like me will sit by and watch him give away our land. There will be a revolt in this country before Rabin will be able to give away any land.

I also don't trust the left-wing partners of Rabin. These Meretz politicians are also too ready to give away our land. I don't blame some of the religious parties for not wanting to join a government with people like Shulamit Aloni who make fun of religion.

I would eventually like a career in the Israeli air force. I am looking forward to serving in the army. I was so proud of my father when I first saw him dressed as a soldier.

He works as a computer specialist for Israel Aircraft. Although he earns less than half of what he earned in the States ten years ago, his salary is considered a good one. Still, we always have to be careful with money. I really want a computer, but my mother tells me that we can't afford one. And we hardly ever get to eat out in restaurants or go on vacations.

When my family came here, my father barely spoke Hebrew. Now he is fluent. All of us kids—there are five of us—are bilingual. We speak English at home and Hebrew at school and with most of our friends.

When I have my own family, I would like to live on a religious settlement somewhere in the territories. Pisgat Ze'ev is a mostly secular neighborhood. I would have preferred growing up in a religious one. I don't like living as a minority. I don't feel that the secular kids accept me. They see us religious kids as weird or different. I felt much more comfortable in Elon Moreh than I feel here in Pisgat Ze'ev.

Still, I am glad to be living in Israel. No matter how difficult my future may be here, I know that this is where I belong and this is where I will stay.

Dalia
(age 17)

I am a
Kibbutznik, but I am also a Jerusalemite. I have lived most of my life here in Kibbutz Ramat Rachel. At one time we were a border settlement. Now, with new neighborhoods like East Talpiot nearby, we have been made a part of Jerusalem.

My family is from Australia. My grandparents in Melbourne were not happy that we left, but my father wanted us to grow up here in a Jewish country. Some of my mother's relatives live here in Israel. The rest are in South Africa and Canada. Dad used to work in a bank back in Australia. Now he works in the kibbutz orchard and he says he is much happier. He's not just a farmer, you know. He does a lot of work with the computerized irrigation system. Mum is over at the nursery most of the time. We girls were such a pleasure to raise that Mum never stopped wanting to work with children.

I was three when we first came to Israel. Three is an important number for me, since I'm the third child in a set of triplets. We're not identical. Believe me, no one even thinks we're related. We even go to different schools. I go to the Givat Brenner School connected to the kibbutz movement. I have to leave here at 6:30 in the morning because the trip takes an hour. My sisters go to schools nearby. One is a regular public school and the other is a trade school. All three of us missed a day of school because of snow last winter.

We don't go to after-school activities at our schools. The kibbutz has so much for us here. The cultural clubs and sports clubs are part of Ramat Rachel's facilities. When I learn to play the recorder, it's expected that I'll be performing in front of visitors. The same goes for people in the dancing and singing clubs. Even if you sign up for tennis or swimming, it is guaranteed that you'll soon be serving kibbutz guests as a tennis teacher or lifeguard. Our kibbutz's main activity is hosting tourists from Israel and all over the world. Everyone in the kibbutz has taken a turn working in the dining room or guest houses—especially in the probation year when newcomers are trying to become kibbutz members.

We are all a big family here. Every birth or death is a pretty big deal. Everything is very different than living in the city. You don't look for jobs and try to earn lots of money. Everyone gets an equal allowance from the whole kibbutz's earnings. So nobody has a house or car or pool that can make the neighbors jealous. No one worries about not having a job or a house or money. Most people get to work in the job that they pick. It's not terrible if someone works in the chicken coop for a couple of years before there is an opening for art teacher or gardener.

Our chicken coops are important. Those long buildings that you pass on the way in contain many thousands of chickens and turkeys. After tourism this is the kibbutz's biggest industry. We are one of the biggest suppliers of poultry for the southern half of Israel. We no longer have our own cows or vegetable patches. Like most kibbutzim we now specialize in one or two things. It sounds funny, but with all those chickens we still have to buy our own eggs. We specialize in eating chickens, not egg-laying chickens.

There are religious services here on Friday night. We don't go. You'll see more tourists from Japan and Germany there than our own kibbutzniks. Our Canadian relatives are religious, but we don't care for that way of life. We are against *haredim* being exempt from the army. It's their country, too. How does their being religious help Israel? I don't know if there's a God. I don't really think about it. Politics is much more important here at Ramat Rachel. You can see all the Rabin and Meretz signs still up from the elections. My parents voted for Labor and we were all happy that Rabin won.

I definitely think that there should be a Palestinian state. They have their rights, too. The Arabs have been here long enough to consider this land to be theirs. What land I would give them is another problem. I don't know where the lines should be drawn. But they won't get their state if they don't behave. We also have to behave, but the *intifada* only prevents peace plans from being considered.

Our kibbutz is close to Bethlehem and smaller Arab villages. Our kibbutz was cut off and almost destroyed in the War of Independence. You can see the memorials and read the plaques at our cemetery up the hill. It is time to stop all the fighting. We try to be good to our neighbors. There are no real problems with Arabs here outside of some vandalism in the orchards.

I don't have any Arab friends. In the eighth grade we went on a class trip to Abu Gosh and hosted Arab kids here. There were no activities after that, so there was no opportunity to keep up any friendships.

We have a few Russian immigrants here. Some travel in to work and three families are now here as members. They are good workers, but they don't seem too willing to fit in like everybody else. We don't have any Ethiopians yet. Almost half of our members came from English-speaking countries, but I don't think there's any prejudice in deciding membership.

We kibbutz kids grow up fast. We are used to responsibility. Almost every girl has boyfriends by the time she gets to seventh grade. I have heard about teenagers on kibbutz getting pregnant, but it has never happened to any of my friends. I don't want to have one serious boyfriend until after the army. Maybe I'll get married at around twenty-one or so. I don't feel that I ought to marry someone on this kibbutz or any kibbutz.

I certainly want to visit other countries. I could live in Toronto or London or anywhere. I'm glad to be here on kibbutz and in Israel, but who knows what the future will bring? There is nothing wrong with people who move out of Israel. And there is nothing forcing me to stay here.

Dan
(age 18)

I was eleven

when I came here from Ethiopia. Things were so strange at the time that it was like I was sleepwalking. My head was always dizzy because things happened so fast. Strange vehicles were whizzing past and people were talking foreign tongues at high speeds. And who ever imagined there were Jews with pale skin?

Everything was much slower back in Gondar Province. Everything was made at home. Preparing and eating meals took up much of the day. I don't ever remember seeing a watch or clock. Father would work the fields and trade in metalwork. Now he is ill and spends most of his time in bed. The trip from Ethiopia to Sudan was very hard on him. We were robbed and beaten. The attacks were not because we were Jewish. All refugees from the fighting were treated this way by gangs of bandits.

We were grateful for the care we received in Sudan. We know that Israel's leaders, Begin and Shamir, and America's President Reagan helped us get to Israel. This is why we voted for Likud. Rabin is not a strong Zionist. And Labor's Golda Meir had said that there are no black Jews. She may have been the prime minister, but she did not know about King Solomon and the queen of Sheba [biblical name for the region of Ethiopia]. In general, the Labor party is not in touch with the Sephardim [Jews from North Africa and Asia] or religious Jews.

The Labor party is back in power and there is more trouble for the Ethiopians. They do not want to allow our relatives who are Falash Mura, forced converts to Christianity, to come here. The government questions their Jewishness, even though they were careful not to marry others. The Russians all married Christians, but the government doesn't mind.

Most Israelis are happy to accept us. We did have some trouble with Israeli kids when we first moved from the Absorbtion Center to Be'er Sheva. It was not hatred, only teasing because we were new and different. My brother and I would respond to the taunts with our fists. We soon won their respect. We moved from Be'er Sheva to the Katamon section of Jerusalem. We did not dream about the Holy Land to live anywhere else. Here in Jerusalem we have plenty of friends of all kinds. We are all active in religious Zionist groups.

My parents would not object if we married religious Jews from another community. My steady girlfriend is Ethiopian, but I have dated non-Ethiopians, too. My parents don't approve of all the freedoms we have with dating. They still live with the ways of the old world. A boy and girl would only meet with introductions by the families. My parents still speak Amharic at home and eat the traditional foods. I am sad to give up some of the old ways. I speak Amharic to my parents and would like my children to keep some of our old customs. I have learned to look people in the eye when I speak to them, even if they are older than me. I have not learned to be loud or to push my way onto buses. In some things I don't want to be too Israeli.

I have an older brother and two sisters. Like my older brother, I am good at auto mechanics. One day perhaps we will have an auto shop together. Right now I am proud to serve in the army like my brother before me. All the difficult training is good for us. It will keep us alive in a time of war. There are only a few nudniks [troublemakers] who give me a hard time for looking different. If they start a fight with me, I make sure they are the ones who look different. Most of the soldiers and officers are warm, like cousins. The hardest part of the army is doing things by a watch all the time.

My brother got a wound on the head from a stone thrown at him while he was serving in Gaza. The army is much too merciful to violent people who break the law. The Israelis should not be afraid to be tough—like the Los Angeles police.

The Jew-haters all criticized Israel for simply throwing four hundred Hamas terrorists into Lebanon. I think this was wrong for another reason. These terrorist leaders were still able to be active in Lebanon, to continue planning the murders of innocent Jews and Arabs. New York learned how dangerous these Hamas fanatics are. Sadly, the Hamas group is in the hearts of most Arabs in Gaza and the West Bank.

The PLO was finished. Arafat was a ghost. But Israel wanted the PLO to stay alive so there would be someone for Rabin to sign a peace treaty with. This treaty is ridiculous. No piece of paper will save Israel from wars against Hamas extremists who are threatening to take over more Arab lands. And if the Israeli army will be given orders to remove Jewish settlers, then there will be many army deserters and maybe a civil war between the right-wingers and the leftists.

Everywhere here there is the feeling of looking out for one another. This is the only home for us. After the army I would love to visit the U.S., Canada, and Japan. If I could visit Ethiopia, I would look for our missing relatives. Only with God's help could they still be alive. Every time I hear about new immigrants, I remember the days of our return to Zion. It took my people two thousand years to get back. But, like they say, "What is time to an Ethiopian?"

Daniella
(age 12)

My mother married one of her students. It was an adult education class in English. My mother was only six years older than my father. I was born in Jerusalem twelve years ago. My mother is also a *sabra*, but she was born in Haifa. My father was born in Poland. He came to Israel when he was twenty-two years old.

Both sets of my grandparents are from Eastern Europe. Only my mother's father is still alive. He lives in Tel Aviv. We go there to see him every couple of weeks. Grandfather lost most of his family in the Holocaust. He himself survived as a partisan fighting in the forests. His friend has a greenish number on her arm where she was branded by the Nazis. When I was little, I asked her about it. I saw that she became uncomfortable. She never really told me what it was. Then, later, I learned about it in school.

All my life I have lived in this house. We have a four-room flat here in Talpiot, in the southeast section of Jerusalem. There is a real mix of people here, Ashkenazim and Sephardim, religious and nonreligious and even some new Russian immigrants. The Ethiopians live further down in East Talpiot.

In the past few years there have been many changes in my neighborhood. People—especially teenagers—come to Talpiot for its nightlife. Just a few blocks from my house there are movie theaters, discos, restaurants, clubs, and Jerusalem's only bowling alley. There's also a new park for children with lots of climbing equipment. And there are new buildings coming up all the time.

I really like my neighborhood. But I don't feel safe here late at night. That is because we are too close to an Arab village. The Arabs who live there cannot be trusted. Maybe I'm a little paranoid, but I won't go out by myself at night. Did you hear about the stabbing a few months back in East Talpiot? A woman was murdered early in the morning while waiting at the bus stop. We are only a seven-minute car ride from the Arab town of Bethlehem, but I've never visited. And I never will. I heard it was a popular place for Jews to go on Friday nights. But that was before the *intifada*.

Mom now works as a rehabilitation teacher for the handicapped. She teaches the blind how to get around. She often goes to their homes. Dad is an electrical engineer. He leaves the house by six and doesn't get home until five or later. He works long hours, but he never complains.

My mother spent many years in America. This summer was my second trip to New York. My mom was frightened by how much this city she lived in went down. So many homeless people on the streets, and many buildings and stores boarded up. And the heat was terrible. It was hard to breathe. San Francisco is five times better, and windier. I didn't see Chicago, but I wanted to because of the Bulls. I love to watch American basketball on TV, but I'm not athletic myself. I'm a bookworm.

I am a real science fiction buff. I have read just about all of L. Ron Hubbard's books in Hebrew translation, and I never miss an episode of "Star Trek." I'm also a fanatic about music. I love Bon Jovi, Guns n' Roses, and the Euro Pop charts on MTV.

During the school year I go to school every day from eight to one. I hated my public elementary school in Geulim. I wasn't popular. I got teased. The kids thought I was weird, so I had to get aggressive. I never did my homework. I was a real devil. Let's just say, I didn't like the teachers. They won't miss me.

Next year for seventh grade I'm going to the Gymnasia school in town. I don't believe in grades. I would probably be better-off in an experimental school. But my boyfriend goes to the Gymnasia school, and I will be depressed if we cannot be together. I've known him since we were two years old. For ten years we are best friends. Yes, it's romantic, too. I don't know if I want to marry him. I only think one day at a time.

I got the chills when the siren went off during the Persian Gulf War. My brother's room was made into the sealed room for defense against a gas attack. When the sirens went off for the Day of Remembrance last spring, I got those chills again.

I think Israel should have retaliated against Iraq instead of letting Saddam fire all those missiles at us. We have one of the best armies in the world. Why not let our enemies know that Jews can no longer be killed by the millions for the fun of it?

The new Labor government is a disaster. Both my parents voted for Labor, but me and my friends support Likud. How can Rabin talk about giving away the Golan? It has much of Israel's water and other natural resources. The Palestinians can be given autonomy, but they can't be trusted to have their own state. Gaza can be theirs, but never East Jerusalem. I couldn't feel any happiness about the peace agreement with the PLO. But it was nice to see the Arabs of Jericho happy for a change. I'm used to seeing them on the news burning tires.

I don't think that the peace agreement between Israel and the PLO is worth very much. Arafat can't make any real promises, because he doesn't represent the Arabs. There will never be any lasting peace with the Arabs because there are too many terrorists among them.

Jerusalem must remain in our hands. The only time that Christians, Jews, and Moslems could go where they wanted in Jerusalem was when Israel was in charge. I would like to see Likud's Netanyahu in power. He knows how to express himself. Not like Shulamit Aloni, who always puts her foot in her mouth and ends up offending everyone, especially the religious Jews.

It gets me real angry that the *haredim* are exempt from the army. That really pisses me off. The *haredim* just stink. They go against everyone. The *haredim* think the roads belong to them. A *haredi* girl my age will look at me like I'm a beast. The *haredim* are like a cult.

I'm not into religion at all. We don't light candles on Shabbat or anything. But we usually have a special chicken dinner on Friday night when we can all eat slowly together. Nobody in the family fasts on Yom Kippur. Once a year we do go into synagogue for a little while to hear the *shofar* [blowing of the ram's horn]. I don't believe in any God. I only believe in science. Christianity makes much more sense to me because they are praying to a person. Jesus is at least something you can see. That I can understand. But what is there to pray to in heaven?

Man made God. God didn't make man. We don't learn about any religion in school. When I have Bible in school, it's nap time. The old-fashioned language is too hard. Who wants to hear an explanation for each word? We hardly talk about religion at home. Not even my grandparents were religious.

I don't judge anybody by religion or background. I could date an Ethiopian if he were my type. I could even date an Israeli Arab, but not a Palestinian from the territories. Too much bad feelings. Not marrying someone because of his religion is racist to me. But it would bother my father if I didn't marry a Jew. So I will probably marry an Israeli Jew and raise my family right here in Talpiot. But I never really think about my future. Who knows if we'll even be here tomorrow?

David
(age 12)

Our house

on Bethlehem Road
is part of the Christ for the
Nations organization and
bible college based in Dallas, Texas. I
was born in Jerusalem in 1982; all
seven of us kids in the family have
lived here all our lives. My youngest
sister is three, and my oldest sister
is twenty-two.

My father was born in
Colombia, South America, but grew
up in the States. Dad was in Israel
first in 1959, but he came to stay in

1966. He remembers driving a classmate home from his Hebrew class on his motor scooter when the Six-Day War broke out. He helped Israelis build bomb shelters during the war.

Just a few months after the war my mother came here on a Christian tour. She was born in Germany and later became an American. When she met my dad, he was working in a Christian bookstore in downtown Jerusalem. He was twenty and she was nineteen.

Now my father is the pastor of the Baptist church on Narkis Street. He also works for the bible college in Dallas, which is why we travel to the U.S. and other places. My mom takes care of the house and the family. There are guests around pretty often, so she's plenty busy.

I like my neighborhood here in Baka. There used to be more empty lots to play in, but now there are many new houses. That's okay, because now there are more kids and nicer parks to play basketball in. I don't play soccer like the Israeli kids, but I go with my older brother to play American football at Sacher Park.

Here in Jerusalem I always feel safe. I can get on a bus and go into town by myself after dark. Anywhere in America my parents would make sure I was with an adult. This country may not have a Disneyland, but it has so much to see. I've gone on some neat hiking trips led by a tour guide who lives upstairs. Even he hasn't seen everything. Egypt is close by and it has some nice things to see. But forget about living there. The Nile River is a toilet. You've got to keep buying bottled water.

Every day my sister and I travel to the Assembly of God school in Shuafat, an Arab village in East Jerusalem. My classmates are mostly Moslem Arabs even though it's a Christian school. I guess they go there because it's a good school and because it doesn't close down every time the *intifada* leaders call a strike. When they closed off the territories, about fifty kids from Ramallah couldn't come in.

The school has got about two hundred students in all. The classes only have from seven to fourteen kids in them. Many of these Arab kids have lived in Detroit or Chicago, so their English is pretty good. The classes are all in English, except for the Arabic class. Arabic is my worst subject. Even the Arab kids don't like this class.

I also had trouble learning Hebrew when I went to the nearby public school for first grade. My favorite subject is math; maybe I'll be a math teacher someday. We have one class a day of Bible studies. All the teachers are American Christians except the Arabic teacher. I'm on the honor roll. A lot of the kids in my classes aren't as smart. This makes it easier for me. I can usually finish my homework in an hour, tops.

I don't think of my Arab classmates as really different. But they pick up things from home. Too many of them have bad feelings about the Jews. Nobody learns Hebrew in our school and almost nobody has any Jewish friends. We don't learn anything in our school that calls this land either Israel or Palestine. When kids tell me that their relatives got thrown in jail by Israeli soldiers, I just figure that they probably were doing something wrong. Israeli soldiers do stop our Arab taxi sometimes for safety reasons. When they see that I don't look Jewish, they know I'm safe in the Arab village. Sometimes I tease my Arab friends by saying that I'm Jewish.

There are very few Christians like us in Israel. Most of the Christians in Jerusalem are Arabs, and their Eastern Orthodox holidays, like Easter, are celebrated at different times than ours. But I don't feel out of place or like a minority here. When kids in my class came over to see my

Christmas tree, they said, "Wow!" They have only seen an American-style Christmas on TV shows like "The Simpsons." On Christmas, Mom plays piano for a choir at Manger Square in Bethlehem.

We have about 250 people worshiping in our church. My best friend goes there. He's half-Japanese and half-Australian. I do wish there were more kids my age at church, but I don't really feel lonely. And it doesn't bother me when most of the country is celebrating Jewish holidays. We have to know about holidays like Yom Kippur because there are no buses running or stores open.

We go to church on Saturday. It doesn't really matter what day is kept as the Lord's Day, as long as people go to church. The people in our church are serious Christians; I guess some of them used to be Moslems or Jews before. I pray a few times a day. Not like the Moslems who bow down to the floor and all, but at meals and special times like that. Our church isn't just for Baptists. I don't really care if some-one's Catholic or Moslem or Jewish. They're all people.

I see you noticed my T-shirt. It says Armageddon Airlines on it. Armageddon is when the world is going to die and be born again after a big fight against the Devil. Israel is where a lot of exciting things are going to happen in the next few years. Armageddon is a real place near the Galilee. The New Testament describes how deep the blood and the dead bodies will be. It might be a nuclear war like it shows on my shirt. But there's nothing to worry about. The good people that get hurt will be okay later. It's up to God what happens to Christians, Jews, and Moslems. The important thing is that soon everybody will know the Lord much better. That's how there will be peace.

The only war I remember is the Persian Gulf War. We all got gas masks, but after the first scud attack we didn't even bother to put them on. Instead, we went up to our roof and videotaped the scuds being hit by Patriot missiles. There's this big flash of light, and you don't hear the bang until a minute later. It wasn't Armageddon, but it was real neat.

My parents don't vote here. They are still American citizens. I don't know much about the political parties, but I don't see how Israel can give up any land. I'm not really sure if Israel would get any peace if they did give up land. Israel is the only land the Jewish people have. The Arabs have lots of big countries all around here and in places like Iraq.

Both my sets of grandparents have come for visits. Everybody loves it here. I don't know why more Americans don't visit here instead of Europe. It's really cool to be in the same places where Jesus walked and performed miracles. It is real special for a Christian to see Nazareth, Bethlehem, the Galilee, and, of course, all over Jerusalem. Some neat things to see near Jerusalem, besides hundreds of famous churches, are the Dead Sea, Hezekiah's water tunnel, and this really cool underground passageway they just opened up under the old Temple of Jerusalem. You won't believe the size of the cornerstone. I've been to the Great Pyramid in Egypt and I can tell you that this stone is about seven times bigger than those.

I've been to Turkey, Holland, and lots of countries in Europe. I like traveling and I love airplanes. I don't get jet-lagged at all. After a trip, when we're finally heading back to Israel, we're all, like, "Yay!" I would like to study at the Christ for the Nations bible college back in Dallas, but I don't think about living anywhere else but in Jerusalem. My older brother wants to volunteer in the Israeli army after college. I might do that, too, but I wouldn't tell that to my Arab classmates.

Dawoud
(age 18)

Is it any wonder why I've wanted to go to Hebrew University since I was a small boy? Every time I look up, I see the campus here on Mount Scopus. Our home is in the valley below, the area called Wadi el Joz. I was born there, but my parents are from Nazareth. My great-grandparents on my father's side, they were from Saudi Arabia. Wars have made my family move from one place to another.

In the difficult years near 1948 some of my relatives fled to Syria. When the fighting was over, it was no longer possible to visit them. The only time I see some of these cousins is when we arrange to meet in London. This only happens every five years.

My mother was born in Lebanon. Most of her family lives in Nazareth, where she grew up. She has relatives who remained in Lebanon. These relatives we have a chance to see because they are in the south, where Israel is in charge. The rest of Lebanon is under Assad of Syria. My father says there is no more Lebanon, that Lebanon died in her long civil war.

Because of Palestinian fighters and now the Hizballah fighters, Lebanon is just a mess. Her army and government are puppets of Syria. You know about all the fighting this last week on the border? The Hizballah want to kill the peace process with Katyusha rockets. The rocket attacks were meant for Christopher [American secretary of state]. But only a peace treaty will get Israel and Syria out of Lebanon. Only peace will give self-determination to Palestinians in Gaza and the West Bank.

My lack of respect for the Hizballah is not because I am Christian and they are Moslems. The problem is that they are fanatics. To them, thousands of refugees and civilian casualties are as nothing. Do you think they were careful not to hurt people in your New York? What if those World Trade Center towers fell down? They only care about their dreams of turning the entire Middle East into one big Iran. This is not the dream of most Arabs. This is their nightmare.

I certainly disapprove of Israel's reaction to the Katyusha attacks. But everyone knew what Rabin would do. For every Israeli who had to run from the Galilee it is known that a hundred Lebanese would have to run from their villages. The situation is difficult because the Hizballah represents Iran, and Iran is very important in the eyes of Syria and others.

The friends you see me with are from my high school. I think there were four of us from our school who are now beginning Hebrew University. My high school was Christian, but we had some Moslem students and teachers, too. When it came to religion, we learned the Bible only, not the Koran. We all learn English. I did well in school, but my favorite subject was recess—playing soccer. Now I am more serious. I would like to be a doctor like my father, so I am taking science courses.

My father sees patients in an East Jerusalem clinic. I would rather do research in a big hospital. I know there is much competition now with all the Russian scientists. I am not worried about getting a job. I will be one of the best, and the best will always be in demand.

My mother is a teacher. She goes back to her native town of Nazareth five days a week. Although we are not strictly religious, we all come in to Nazareth for Christian holidays and stay with family. For these several days the small town is almost as busy as Jerusalem. Tourists come in by the bus-loads. They come from Denmark, Japan, Nigeria—everywhere in the world. Nazareth has a campaign to build more hotels, to widen narrow streets, and to have more attractive shops by the year 2000.

I just broke up with my girlfriend. We were together for three years. She was a little old-fashioned for me. She expect-ed me to spend too much time with her family. And I am not ready to get married for many years. My father was thirty when he got married. Now that I am in college, I could meet many girls. I know that my parents would accept a girl that I chose from any background. Maybe my grandparents would complain, but they don't have power over my life. I am not an unskilled laborer from a small village. My family is very modern.

My area was not affected by the *intifada*. My school did not close down. I even know some graduates from my school who volunteered in the Israeli army. As citizens they had this choice. This is never a choice most of my friends would consider. I don't dislike Israel or the army at all. But serving in the Israeli army could mean fighting against my own people. This cannot be done. Those Arabs who do serve in the army do not have a future profession like me. They want an easy life, maybe working for the government when the army is over.

My family voted for the Labor party. I don't agree with my friends that all the Israeli parties are bad. Rabin could bring peace because he is realistic about security problems. I think that Rabin has been too harsh, however. When he expelled the Hamas leaders to Lebanon, this was cruel to their families. Better to put them in a jail here where at least they could be visited by their wives and children and mothers.

I would like to see a Palestinian country with open borders to Israel. Without this kind of real cooperation between the countries a peace treaty would not be good. I want this Palestinian state to have a real democracy, just like in Israel. I would like the PLO in charge, but a new generation of leaders. I don't want Arafat as a dictator or a president. When nobody listens to him, he lets the violent groups get people's attention.

A Palestinian state in East Jerusalem and the West Bank should be free of violence. In Gaza there is a bigger problem with Hamas. The Jews also have problems with religious fundamentalists. Some of them throw stones to stop traffic on the Jewish sabbath. There is a way to keep very religious Jews and Moslems and Christians happy. They must have respect from any government. After all, this is Jerusalem and a Holy Land for all of these religions.

If Arafat or Husseini [head of the Palestinian delegation at the peace talks] would be the leader of a Palestinian state, they must be more respectful of religion. They also must not use religion for political reasons or to bring in armed fanatics. Either way would bring only war. We need a good peace. A peace that could bring Palestinians out of the refugee camps and back from other countries where they have fled.

I am not happy that Israel is getting a half million new Jews from Russia, Ethiopia, and elsewhere. But they are refugees, too. I understand that people running from war must have a place to go. Look at the thousands of new buildings that went up in Jerusalem in my lifetime. Certainly there is room for Arab and Jewish refugees here. All you need are good scientists and good peacemakers.

Efrata
(age 17)

This country
would be wonderful . . . if we could only get rid of the Arabs, the *haredim*, and the Russians.

As for the Arabs, I wouldn't give them anything, not even autonomy. It's not a state that they want. It's the whole land of Israel. And don't think they'll settle for less. If I were running this country, not a single Arab would be employed here. Why hire an Arab? So he can stab you in your back? As far as I'm concerned, they can all leave and settle in any one of their twenty-two countries.

And they can take the *haredim* with them. Who needs these parasites? Why should they be given any of this state's benefits when they don't do anything for it? Three wars my father has fought in. He's in the Golani Brigade. The best. In the Yom Kippur War he was badly wounded, with his whole body in a cast. And on the last day of the shooting he lost his brother. Almost every family I know has lost someone dear so that we may live in a Jewish state. It's time for the *haredim* to make some sacrifices, too. Don't you agree?

As for the Russians, what good are they? They've been here for less than two years, and suddenly they can vote. Now they put Labor in power. They're getting all kinds of benefits, and still they protest. The Ethiopians are given less. And do they ever complain? The Ethiopians, at least, had the sense of gratitude to vote for Likud. When my parents and grandparents came here from Morocco, they were put into tents. They never asked for anything.

Now my father has a good job in computers, and my mother's a secretary. My parents worked hard for everything they have. On their own they were able to buy a four-room apartment here in East Talpiot. No one gave them anything. But the Russians expect everything to be handed to them. And there are too many of them for this small country. My sister just finished army service, and the job that she wanted was given to a new Russian immigrant. Now, is that right?

Don't get me wrong. I love this country. I would never want to leave Jerusalem. Now with movies and more restaurants open on Shabbat it is better than ever. I have a serious boyfriend whom I met in a disco. He's twenty and still in the army. His family is from Tunisia and he knows a lot about electronics. I don't know if we'll get married. I wouldn't even want to get married till I'm twenty-five. But when I do have a family, this is where I would want to raise my children.

I now live with a brother and two sisters. We all go to state schools. I like history and English, but not enough to go on to university. What good is it? Do you think I want a boring desk job? Besides baby-sitting, I work part-time in a pub. I'm really too young for such a job, but I have, you know, *protectzia* [influential contacts]. After the army I'd like to go to the Far East. I have no real interest in the area. It's just the cool place to go right now.

In my neighborhood and in town everyone gets along. There are no problems between Sephardi and Ashkenazi or between religious and nonreligious. I myself am not religious. I'm an atheist. I just don't believe in God. To me the Torah is a bunch of fairy tales, made-up stories. I have no reason to believe any of it is true. My parents light candles on Shabbat. I won't bother with it. I no longer fast on Yom Kippur either. But religious people don't bother me. My own grandparents are religious. I just don't want them to tell me what to do and how to live my life. To each his own. And I'm left pretty much alone.

Ephraim
(age 13)

When

my grandparents first came to Israel from Yemen, their lives were horrible. They were put into small, smelly tents in a transit camp in Haifa. All they were given was a blanket and a plastic tub. To take a shower, they had to fill the tub with water and pour it over their heads. "Now we live like kings," my grandmother tells us.

My grandparents and most of my family still live in Haifa, but ten years ago my parents moved to French Hill in Jerusalem. Five years later we moved to a bigger apartment in Pisgat Ze'ev.

When we were new in the neighborhood, I had some trouble with the Ashkenazi kids. I got beaten up a few times. But once I let the bullies know that I could fight back, it ended. Now my best friend is Ashkenazi.

I go to a religious school near the Old City. There are about thirty boys in my class. My favorite subject is *Gemorah* [Talmud], because the teacher makes it so interesting. I fall asleep every day during math. So I like that class, too. It's my break. The school day ends at five, but we have time in school to do our homework. So after supper I usually have some free time. That's when I play with my computer or visit my friend. Sometimes when I get bored I watch TV, even though my *rebbes* [rabbis] tell me that it is forbidden.

I would like to go to Europe. But just to visit. I want to live my whole life here in Jerusalem. Who wouldn't want to live here? Isn't it every Jew's yearning to come here? I can't imagine any land more beautiful than ours.

This place would be a Gan Eden [Garden of Eden] if it weren't for the Arabs. On the way home from work my father's car gets stoned almost every day. My father has to face that after working hard all day in the hot sun as a tank mechanic for the army. And my bus to school by the Old City also gets stones thrown at it.

A stone is a deadly weapon. Didn't David kill Goliath with a stone? The *intifada* would have ended a long time ago if we had responded to their stones with our own stones. We need to treat the Arabs the same way they treat us. What they do to us, we should do back. There is no other solution.

There is no way we can give up any of our land. It is our land, and not theirs. If we give the Arabs a little, they will want more and more. Rabin is a fool if he thinks otherwise. It is not possible to be friends with Arabs. You cannot trust them. They will act like your friend, but then they will stab you in the back.

Peres and Rabin had the *chutzpah* [nerve] to quote from the Torah about peace during this agreement with the PLO. I have a better quote, from Jeremiah: "[They cry] 'Peace, peace' and there is no peace." At the same moment that the peace agreement was being sealed, an Israeli soldier was stabbed in Gaza. We can't make peace with *goyim* [gentiles]. I have been participating in Habad-sponsored demonstrations against this dangerous peace.

Rabin is not listening to the people. He should resign. Rabin is not negotiating a give-and-take with the Arabs—only a give-and-give. Gaza and Jericho is only the beginning. It is crazy to throw away land to an enemy when we have such a tiny country. Where will we live? Where will Jewish immigrants from Russia or anywhere else have a place to live? Rabin shook the hand of Arafat! How can a person even stand near such an evil murderer?

The only Arab I've ever spoken to is the one who works in our *makolet* [grocery store]. He is fine, but I know that you can never trust a *goy*.

If I could have voted in the election, I would have voted for *Shas* [religious Sephardi party]. People are so quick to accuse its party members of corruption and thievery. But nothing has ever been proven. Isn't a person innocent until proven guilty? The Ashkenazim, especially, are so hasty to judge. I can honestly say that if it weren't for the politicians, I wouldn't feel any tension these days between the Ashkenazim and the Sephardim. Not in my neighborhood, and not in my school.

I welcome all the Russian immigrants. It doesn't matter whether they are religious or not. They will help build our country. But I have one question: Why were they allowed to vote in the election? Many of them have been here for less than a year. And they all voted for Labor and Meretz. Just because the Ethiopians voted for Likud, they voted for Labor. Now does that make sense?

I don't know whether I will serve in the army or learn Torah full-time. Everything is from Heaven. But I do know that I am already more religious than my parents. My mother does not cover her hair. I would expect my wife to. A head covering is more than just a symbol of modesty. Quite honestly, I don't think I could marry an Ashkenazi. One of my cousins did, and everyone in the family loves and accepts her. But I want to marry one of my own. A Taimani [Yemenite], just like my mom. But more religious.

Gina
(age 15)

I have been living in Israel now for a year and a half. I was born in Baku. It is a hot, humid city close to the Baltic Sea. There are only two thousand Jews in a town of two million. Most of the people who live there are Moslems. When my parents were growing up, Baku was a safe place for Jews. But as the economy began to fall apart, rivalries began to develop between the different ethnic groups. Jews became an easy scapegoat. My parents felt that they had to leave.

We came straight to Pisgat Ze'ev from Ben-Gurion Airport. Friends of ours who had already emigrated from Russia were living here. They liked the neighborhood, and they found our apartment for us.

I much prefer my life here. There are no tensions in my neighborhood and everyone makes us feel welcome. When we first came here, there were so many people eager to help us. Strangers came to our house with clothes, food, and even furniture. They made us feel as though they really wanted us here. Everybody is like one big family. In Russia hardly anybody tries to help anyone else.

In my native town I always stood out. I was the only Jew in my class. I had tried to make myself as invisible as possible. But still everyone knew that I was Jewish. And that was an uncomfortable feeling.

Even though I had to learn a new language, I adjusted easily to life here. School is easier here and the school day is shorter. My teachers are better. After I finish high school, I will serve in the army. The army will be good for me. And I will be happy to give back something to Israel.

The behavior of the Jews here amazes me. I had to be so meek in the Soviet Union just to survive. Here the Jewish kids have so much *chutzpah*. I am so happy to be in a country where I don't have to try to hide my identity. All my friends are happy here, too.

But the adjustment has been more difficult for our parents. Most of our parents were professionals in Russia. The status their jobs brought them was the only way they felt important. They are used to working in professions that are highly respected. It is difficult for all of them to find jobs in their fields here in Israel. And many of them feel that they are not given enough respect.

My father was an engineer in Russia, and just last month he finally found a position as an engineer here in Israel. So he was out of work for almost a year and a half. My mother was a literature teacher at a university. But here she is running a private day care center in our apartment. I know she would rather teach literature. But still, she doesn't complain. I am always reading in the papers about Russian immigrants who complain about life here and want to go back to their native country. But I know of only one person who considers returning to Russia. And she wouldn't be happy anywhere. All of my friends here are happy.

Now with Labor in power I hope there will be a new era of peace with our Arab neighbors. My parents voted for Meretz because they feel that the Palestinians should be given their own state. I agree. I don't think Israel should give up Jerusalem or the Golan Heights, but the West Bank and Gaza belong to the Palestinians. Giving Gaza to the PLO was a smart thing.

We also support Meretz's platform that calls for the separation of religion and state. We are not religious. I was taught in Russia that religion is evil. And now, even though I don't think it is evil, I think that it is senseless. I've been to a synagogue a few times here in Israel. And the experience is meaningless. I can't imagine that religion would ever hold any attraction for me. The religious parties just seem to argue with one another. I would like to see buses riding on Shabbat and stores open, because it is the only day that we are off. I feel like somewhat of a prisoner here in Pisgat Ze'ev on Shabbat.

Despite this, I am happy to be living as a free Jew in a Jewish state. I wouldn't want to live elsewhere.

Leah
(age 14)

I spent the first nine years of my life in Monsey, New York. There the world consisted of *frum* [religious] Jews and *goyim*. When we came to Israel, we were shocked to discover Jews who lived like goyim.

If it weren't for my grandfather, we would still be in Monsey. But my grandfather, a well-known *rav* [rabbi], needed my father to serve as a *dayan* [judge]. So five

■ *73* ■

years ago we moved to Har Nof, a western suburb of Jerusalem.

The adjustment has been most difficult for my mother. She misses all her friends in Monsey. All of her family is still in the States. Back home she had a good job as a teacher in a nearby yeshiva. Here she doesn't work. And although we kids keep her busy—there are ten of us—she acts like she's lonely. I know that she wants to go back. She tells that to my father, but he says he's happy here.

I, myself, have mixed feelings. I like being able to go to the Kotel [Western Wall]. When I was in yeshiva in Monsey, that used to be my dream. But there isn't much else I like here.

I much preferred my yeshiva in America. The teachers were friendlier and more understanding. If my mother sent a note explaining why I didn't do my homework, it would be accepted. Here the teachers don't even want to look at notes. They scream at you if you aren't prepared. I'm lucky that I'm a good student, or it would be unbearable.

When I started fourth grade here, nobody welcomed me. All the girls stared at me. They made fun of my accent. They looked down on me because I was a foreigner. The girls in Monsey never acted that way to a newcomer. They all had *midot* [good characteristics] and *derech eretz* [good manners]. It seems as though living in Israel hardens you.

I also don't like the tensions between the Ashkenazim and Sephardim here. Especially before the elections. Just outside his *yeshiva*, two Shas boys attacked my brother and broke his finger because he is an Ashkenazi with *payis* [sidelocks]. They told him that they were beating him up because people like him support Agudah. He is only ten years old. And my father didn't even vote. He says that the politicians in this country don't do anything anyway, so why bother voting for

The Persian Gulf War was really frightening. Our friends from America kept on calling every time they heard of a missile attack. Do you know what it's like to get a family of ten kids into a sealed room with gas masks on while the phone is ringing?

I think things have gotten out of hand with the Arabs. At the beginning of the *intifada,* Israel should have taken much stronger measures. No matter what Israel does, the world condemns her. She must start thinking about doing what's right for her. Israel lost so many lives for this land. Does she have to lose any more? When the Arabs fled in 1948, they lost their claim to this land. No one forced them to leave. That was their choice. No one forced them to attack us. Is it our fault that they lost? This is the only land we have for Jews escaping from persecution everywhere.

Last year my oldest sister, who is eighteen, returned to the States. Maybe I will do the same in a few years. I would like to marry someone who sits and learns Torah all day. I would prefer that he doesn't have to work. And I would like to live in either Monsey or Borough Park, Brooklyn.

Leonid
(age 14)

When I was living in Moscow, I was teased all the time because I am Jewish. The Russian kids used to say to me, "This is not your country. Why don't you leave?" I never answered them. I was afraid to. There is hateful graffiti on subway walls blaming Jews for everything. I could not even go into a grocery store without someone yelling out at me, "Zhid."

I came to Israel two years ago from Moscow. I am now living in a three-room apartment in Neve Ya'akov with my mother. We are sharing our flat with two single men who are also new Russian immigrants. My father will be joining us in another month. He is still working in Russia.

Here in Israel I don't feel such pressures or dangers. There are no groups of schoolchildren teasing me. And I can say whatever I want.

Here we have a voice in the way our country is run. I feel that the Arabs who don't like it here should leave. Why don't the stone throwers go to Iraq? Isn't Saddam Hussein their big hero? I don't like sharing a tiny land with people who would be happier if I were dead.

The peace agreement between Israel and the PLO puts the entire state of Israel in danger. How could Israel even think of giving up Jericho? I can understand giving the Arabs autonomy in Gaza, but Jericho belongs to us. And now there's talk of giving the Golan to Syria. What about our kibbutzim? And what about our national security?

I don't think the Arabs should be given a state here in Israel. Soon they will want all of Jerusalem. Don't they have enough states of their own? We Jews must have our own state. The anti-Semitism in this world leaves us no other choice.

I find the religious life here interesting. I always say to my mother now, "Why didn't you teach me anything about being Jewish?" My mother tells me that it was too hard to live a religious life in Russia. In the time of Stalin, if a Jew was found with a *tallit* [prayer shawl], he was murdered. Right before I made aliyah, my grandmother gave me a tallit that belonged to my grandfather. She had been hiding it for over forty years.

Maybe someday I'll be religious. I no longer eat pork or

food that isn't kosher. And I would like to give my children a religious education. Let them have a real choice how to live inside and out. This is the kind of freedom we never had.

My biggest difficulty here has been with the school system. I was placed in a public school in Neve Ya'akov, but I didn't like the school. The classes were crowded, and the teachers didn't know how to teach. There are no high schools yet in nearby Pisgat Ze'ev. But I knew from my friends that there were better schools than the one I was assigned to. So I told the principal in Neve Ya'akov that I wasn't going to school anymore until a better placement was found for me. So for six months I stayed at home and taught myself. I studied Hebrew and English and math.

My poor mother almost had a nervous breakdown. She was always screaming at me to go back to my crummy school. But I knew how to get what I wanted. I tell you, it pays to have *chutzpah* in this country. I just found out yesterday that I will be going to a top school in San Simeon this coming term. If I hadn't gotten this, I would have continued to study at home and, with the help of tutors, prepare for the *bagrut* exams to complete high school.

Most of my friends are also Russian immigrants. Mostly we get together in each other's houses when our parents aren't home and we listen to music. My favorite group is Guns n' Roses. I don't have girlfriends yet. There is time for that when I get older.

After army service I would like to go to the Hebrew University and study medicine. Both my parents are doctors.

About five years ago many of my relatives left Moscow for the United States. Every time they wrote to us, they told us to go to Israel instead of the U.S. I'm glad we made that choice. I hope to be able to raise my family right here in Jerusalem.

Liat
(age 15)

My father's

family came to this country from Cairo, and my mother's from Algiers. My grandfather tells me when he was a young man in Cairo, he always wore a *fez* while riding buses. From time to time the Jews would not be allowed to ride buses or they would suddenly be asked to get off. With a *fez* on his head no one could tell my grandfather was Jewish.

I was born in Bet Shemesh

fifteen years ago. Now I live in Pisgat Ze'ev, a northeast suburb of Jerusalem. I prefer my new neighborhood because it is closer to the center of Jerusalem and it's not as hot as Bet Shemesh. Pisgat Ze'ev has an ideal mix of all people, and everyone gets along. Even though I am religious, I would not want to live in a neighborhood where everyone is religious. That would be too much. If one is strong in her beliefs, one can live anywhere. In fact, in the past few years I've become even more observant.

I attend a religious high school in Ramat Eshkol. It has won awards for academic excellence and is very demanding. It has a reputation to keep up. But I don't mind the pressure. It's good for me. My favorite subjects are Bible and math. Maybe I will be an accountant like my mother.

When I have free time, I stock shelves in the supermarket. I work for a wholesaler. I don't mind the work and I like earning my own money. I'm also preparing to be a B'nai Akiva [religious Zionist] counselor. I will soon be leading my own group on Tuesday afternoons and on Shabbat.

When I finish high school, I will have a choice between doing national service or army service. All religious girls are given that choice. My sister is doing national service, but I am looking forward to serving in the army and seeing more of the country.

I am afraid there will always be an army in Israel. I don't think we will ever be able to live in peace with the Arabs. They cannot be trusted. The Arabs talk peace, but they murder us. We have an Arab neighborhood down the road from us, but I myself have never spoken to anyone there.

This land belongs to the Jews. The Torah gave it to us and commanded us to live in it. We are not permitted to give it away. Rabin has no right to speak for us. He is a traitor. I don't know how he can shake hands with someone who has vowed to destroy us. There can never be a Palestinian state on any part of our land.

I don't expect the Palestinians to disappear. They do the work the Jews won't do. Jews like to work with their heads, not their hands. The new Russian immigrants are not about to do hard labor. They have too much *seichel* [sense] to do the work the Arabs do. So we have no choice but to continue to employ them.

The people now in power couldn't care less about us. They only care about themselves. And that is one of Israel's biggest problems—its politicians.

Only God can save the Jewish people. Hopefully, God will soon awaken the leftists in this country to reality, before they give it all away, piece by piece for a peace that can never be.

Limor
(age 16)

"The Young and the Restless." That's my favorite show. I watch TV whenever I'm bored. Which is often. I learned all my English from the TV. Do you think I could learn so good from school? Now, on summer vacation, I'm usually hanging out here in Jerusalem's outdoor mall at night. They don't let me into the discos and bars on Yoel Solomon Street yet. But I like to hang out nearby.

Those bottles? Don't worry.

The guys are just throwing them to hear the crash. What did you think? It was petrol bombs from Arabs? These punks aren't hurting anybody. They're my friends. No, they aren't trying to make a point. It's just something to do.

Some of my friends take drugs. Hashish. Cocaine. But I don't know the real heroin guys, the ones who use needles. I live in Kiryat Yovel, southwest of here. It's a pretty poor section. The city is making improvements. It's a lot less dumpy. The worst of the changes is all the new Russians.

The Russians fight with the Moroccans. I swear, people just don't like the Russians. They have their own little gangs. And they smell bad. They take all the money and all the jobs. You can believe me because I'm Russian, too. At least my parents were born there. They came here twenty-three years ago, so I don't feel close to these smelly newcomers.

There was no Russian spoken at home. There was no home. My father, that bastard, left my mother twelve years ago. What do me and my sister have left? I have an old, sick grandfather next door. I see my father sometimes, but he won't even nod. I don't want to talk about it.

School? *That* you want to talk about?! I'm being kept back in the tenth grade. I'm not stupid. The teachers are out to get us. There are forty kids in a room. Nobody cares about you. I wouldn't go at all if my mother didn't force me. I can't say I like anything—maybe history. My grandmother's side went through the Holocaust and the camps. I've read some books about the *Shoah* [Holocaust]. But I'd really like to study design. I don't know if I'm any good, but I enjoy making new fashions.

I'm stuck in my dumb school from eight in the morning to twelve or two in the afternoon. I only go to meet hunks. I've got lots of boyfriends. Most of the guys that come over to kiss me are not even in my school. I know them from town.

We had an argument the other day about how many virgins there are in my class. The guys said only 5 percent of the girls are still virgins. I said it was closer to 40 percent. What the hell do boys know? They only know what they want.

Most of the girls who get pregnant have abortions. It's a pain. And it's expensive, too. I don't ever want to get married or have children. Do I want to sit home cleaning up peepee all day? I won't need a guy for his money. I work in a toy store after school. I make seven shekels an hour. In the summer I work almost twelve hours a day. I don't spend it all on myself. I give some to my mother.

The police here are no good. They are too harsh with kids. They always suspect us of bad things. Why don't they go bother the Arabs? The Labor government is no good. They want to give up our land for a promise. A promise from Arabs?! That's why I prefer Tsomet or Moledet. The Arabs should be thrown into the sea. Let them lie to the fish. Let them bargain with the fish. Let them stab the fish. Rabin's government is good for nothing. My mother voted for Rabin.

There are plenty of problems with the ultrareligious *haredim*. The *haredim* are stupid, and they live a stupid life. They have no idea what they're doing. They deny their children a normal life. Their kids learn nothing, not even how to speak the language of the country. It's not fair that they don't serve in the army. It's a lie that they can't study and be in the army. They just want us to fight for them. So they can stay home and eat their gefilte fish.

The religious keep the buses from going on Shabbat. That's the only thing better about Tel Aviv. Do I believe in anything? Sure. I believe in anarchy. We have to get rid of things like school. Let it be voluntary. Let everybody decide for themselves what they want to learn. Let the army be voluntary. Maybe I'd go. Just to meet hunks.

Louis
(age 15)

My house

is one building away from the Via Dolorosa. These holy streets in the Christian Quarter of the Old City are where I played as a child and where I come now to look for my friends. I was born on the Street of the Chain at the edge of the Jewish Quarter. My parents and two sisters moved to a four-room apartment here after my father got a job for the United Nations in Vienna. My parents were also born here in the Old City, but my father's parents came from Nazareth. My mother's side is from Jordan. My Jordanian grandmother tells us how she was almost killed by a mortar shell in 1967.

My mother is not typical at all. She goes in to West Jerusalem four days a week and works as a receptionist in a government health clinic. She has been criticized for being too modern, and even too Israeli. She tells them to mind their own business.

I go to the French school near the New Gate. The De La Salle school starts at 8:00 and gets out at 2:15. Most of the students are Christian Arabs, but there are some Moslems and Armenians, too. The school is expensive because it is private. Tuition is seven hundred dollars a year. I'm finished after next year. Besides French, we learn English, Latin, and German. Add these to Arabic and Hebrew and I know five languages. If I don't do something with my interest in computers, I could always work for a place where my languages are valuable.

I don't know why I should be excited about the change in Israeli politics. Politicians are always promising things like a merchant in the *souk* [market]. After you buy, you know you are cheated. Nothing is changing for our people but the slogans on the wall. Before the *intifada* I did not feel any hatred between the Jews and Arabs here. Now I feel that the Jews hate us. I imagine they feel our hatred as well. The *intifada* was very hard on most of my friends. They have shops that depend on tourist income. Not only were many tourists frightened away, but shops were often closed after the morning. Without sales, many had to depend on money from Saudi Arabia and the PLO that went to the families of martyrs and heroes of the *intifada*.

My family didn't vote in the Israeli elections. They

couldn't. After 1967 they were offered Israeli citizenship, but they decided to keep up their ties to Jordan.

We get along well with Moslem Arabs. We don't usually socialize with people in the Moslem Quarter, however. If we are there, we are walking through for business.

I am against Jews moving into the Moslem Quarter. It is illegal. They are coming in and taking these homes. I don't think they are really buying them. It could also be that the sellers are not the real owners.Those who sell such homes are robbers. In any case, the Jews have no right to live there.

If each community stays within its bounds, there could be peace. If there would be less soldiers around, there would be less boys throwing rocks. Things have been back to normal these past few months. The *intifada* was bad for children as well as storekeepers. The flow of our studies was interrupted.

We also missed days of school with the Persian Gulf War. For the first attack my family also put on gas masks. Who knew if the destruction would be wide or narrow? Soon we knew that Saddam was after the Jewish capital, Tel Aviv. He would never attack Jerusalem. Saddam was foolish for seizing Kuwait. I don't admire his leadership at all, but we all admire his courage for attacking Israel. Israel did not get into another war because she was getting more financial and propaganda benefits for sitting still.

Saddam may not be finished yet. But he is not the Messiah reborn. My family looks to Arafat for leadership. I know all the charges that he is corrupt and secular, but I don't believe them. Habash makes violence a religion, and Hamas's religion is violence. My parents are devout Christians who are opposed to any violence. I might be even more religious than my parents. I would like a church school for my children.

Even the merchants who bargain all day with customers

are serious about their religion. In the Christian Quarter one doesn't see immorality. Some of the poorer teenagers have become involved in drugs. I'm sure the drug suppliers and most of the clients are Jews. There is one Jewish woman who sells drugs and is a prostitute. She doesn't dare to operate in the Old City—only in Jewish Jerusalem.

I have never been arrested, but most of my friends have been. Unlike me, they don't sit at home with a computer when school has been closed down by the *intifada*. They throw stones, burn cars, and get into confrontations with soldiers and police. When they are detained, they face hours of sitting in darkness and fear. Many times their hands are tied to the ceiling. The authorities are careful to hit them where no bruises can be seen by the court. They also make the prisoners swear upon their family's life that they will reveal nothing of their incarceration. It's an average of two years for stone throwing. Attempted murder is the charge.

The new flood of Soviet immigrants has made the whole situation much worse. I do not deny that there are places for Jews to live in this land. But the Arab people here must not be outcasts.

There are many winds blowing different clouds over the horizon. One of these storm clouds is thundering for a Palestinian state. This state should include East Jerusalem, the West Bank, and Gaza. It should have room for the Palestinian Diaspora, whose generations are subsisting on U.N. charity. Right now I'd say that a Palestinian state is just a cloud, a dream. I don't see it happening in my generation.

I wouldn't mind studying in Europe for a few years. I have been to several cities on the continent, and I'd love to see the U.S. But I wouldn't pick up and leave for good. Jerusalem is my home.

Mark
(age 14)

I am used to living with Moslems. Only a year and a half ago I was living in Dagestan. This is a Moslem republic in the former U.S.S.R. It is near the Caspian Sea. We lived in the capital city of this cattle-raising area. There were more Jews in the nearby city of Dahrbent. I'm reminded of that medieval walled city every time I see the walled Old City here in Jerusalem.

Of the million or so people in

Dagestan only about thirty thousand were Jews. The Jews never suffered pogroms or any harsh restrictions. There are thirty-two different ethnic groups there, so the Jews didn't stick out too much. Still, about half the Jews have left. About a third of the Jews have married Moslems. The Sephardic Jews of the area were there for many centuries. I guess they came there soon after the expulsion from Spain in 1492. We were Ashkenazim who came later.

My father's grandparents were from White Russia. My father's father served in the red army during World War II. Because he was on the Iran-Iraq border and not on the front with Germany, the government did not give him the honors and money he deserved. On my mother's side my grandparents were from Moldavia and the Ukraine. They lost most of their family in the Holocaust.

My mother was an accountant and my father was a photographer. They were not wealthy, but I never heard of money or job problems back in Dagestan. While my mother gets the language and accounting training she needs here, she is earning money taking care of old people in private homes. She talks Yiddish and Russian on these jobs, so she doesn't get to speak much Hebrew. My father is now pruning trees in the Jerusalem Forest for the Jewish National Fund. It's not permanent, but he will do anything until he can set up a photo shop. He insisted we move to Jerusalem because it is so beautiful here for taking photos. But he tells us he can't feed us on the scenery.

Even our journey was less dangerous than our first few weeks in Israel. My older brother and I were staying in the north at a student *ulpan* [language institute]. Katyusha rockets were fired from Lebanon and a young immigrant was killed. It was a shock to us, but no one was ready to leave the country. The security zone that Israel has in southern

Lebanon is clearly not big enough. Let Israel leave Lebanon or other territories only after five years go by without attacks.

My mother also preferred that we move to Jerusalem. It is safer than the north and not hot in the summer like the towns near the Mediterranean. We have friends living in Jerusalem who put us up until we got this apartment in Baka. We have one room less than we used to have, but I don't mind. My older brother will be out of the house often because he is starting Hebrew University.

On our street there is a good-size park with a place to play basketball and soccer. The kids are playing with me more and more, but they still don't want to know my name. They call me Gingy, the Israeli name for anyone with red hair.

I was teased a bit in school when I first came. With two certain boys in my class the teasing was not in fun. We fought after school and one of them ended up in the hospital. My uncle taught me boxing pretty well. The police were involved and my family was upset. I was only defending myself; the boys themselves admitted this. I don't have enough good friends who are Israelis, but at least I don't have any more enemies.

I don't have a real girlfriend yet. When I date, I don't think I will date Sephardi girls. They laugh too loud at things I don't find funny. I will probably marry a girl from my own background. But, for the right girl, I will learn some French or English if she doesn't speak Hebrew well.

I really like zoology, but I'm not so sure what I could do in that field. I'm good with computers and I'm learning electronics. If I have the opportunity to postpone the army for university, like my brother, I would do so.

My parents voted, but we were here for too little time to know what we were doing. None of us at our *ulpan* knew what each party stood for. But a man from the Labor party offered all the adults there fifty shekels to vote for his party. So my parents took the money and voted like all the rest. I don't blame them. Later I learned that the Likud party worked to get us out of our country. Also, soon after the election Labor took away the money grants to immigrants. Now we have loans instead. If there would be a party for Soviet *olim* [immigrants] we will vote for it.

In Dagestan the only thing Jewish we had was our identity. On Passover we had some matzo, but we didn't even know not to eat bread at the same time. We are learning a little here what it means to be Jewish. My cousin has become religious and wears a *kipa* [skullcap]. He enjoys learning in a *yeshiva*. We are happy that he is happy, but I don't understand why someone prays.

Maybe there is a God. This idea answers questions but it asks questions. Are we amusing some great being in this fishbowl of the universe? My cousin says the Jews are chosen to teach the world. The Moslems and the Christians say they are the real chosen ones. Then they all kill each other. They all want Jerusalem. This is why the Soviets taught that religion is only more evil competition between people.

I don't have a problem with no buses on Shabbat or with the *haredim*. Why not respect their beliefs? They have a strong love for family and children so they are not bad people. When you see them dance, like at a wedding, they are as drunk as any real drunks—but with no vodka. This is special, this power. Let them have their streets without cars on the Shabbat, and let the Arabs have rule over themselves.

But we should not give to the Arabs land like the Golan Heights. This is crazy. I saw those mountains up north. Whoever is in the Golan is controlling half of the land. Israel is much too small. It is hard for someone from the U.S.S.R. to find it on a map.

Muhammad
(age 14)

When I am

not at school I can always be found selling hot corn here in Liberty Bell Park. I usually sell to other Arabs and to Israelis. The tourists don't buy from me. They eat better things in their big hotels.

I live close by in the Abu Tor section of East Jerusalem. This area below the Old City is like two separate neighborhoods. The Jews are on the hill in big new homes. We Arabs are down below in older homes. I like to ride my bike on the Jewish street because it is smooth and new. My street is full of holes that nobody in the city cares about fixing.

My mother and I were both born there, but my father came from Hebron. He moved here after the 1967 war to get Israeli citizenship and a construction job. Father drives a cement truck and dump trucks full of building sand.

There are eight of us living in a two-room house. One of our rooms used to be half the size. One night twenty friends and relatives came and moved the wall halfway into our yard. The sides were quickly built up, and old tiles of the same color were put on the new roof. The chicken coop, the benches, even an olive tree was moved over to look just like the old yard. The inspectors and police never noticed the change. This is how we live, on cleverness.

If the new walls were discovered, they would have been knocked down. You have to do things secretly because the authorities never give permission to build. Only hospitals or schools get built near us, but not places to live.

I used to go to a very strict Jordanian school near the Jaffa Gate. There were no girls or even women teachers. Worst of all, the teachers were quick to hit us for not knowing the lessons. I had to get out of there. The only way was telling my father that I wanted a more religious school. Now I go to the Al-Aksa school near the Dome of the Rock. There are more hours in the new school, but there is more prayer and less study. No teachers hit me there. They probably would hit me if they knew that I didn't pray when I wasn't in school.

Much of the last few years of school was ruined anyway. The schools were closed for long periods during the *intifada*. I don't care for school, but this trouble was good for nobody. Who wants to be free from school when you are stuck at home with curfews? I didn't run with the *shabab* [politicized youth gangs]. In fact, I was friendly with the Border Patrol. Most of them are Druze who used to live in Lebanon. I practiced my French with them. We traded fresh water for chocolate. Because they knew I was friendly with the Druze, the *shabab* left me alone. If any of my friends were arrested, they knew I could help them out.

During the Persian Gulf War my parents did seal a room. We put on gas masks, too. I did not cheer for Saddam. He will not bring peace. I only want quiet and good relations with everyone in Jerusalem. I did not follow the elections, but maybe there is a greater chance for peace now. My parents did not want to vote. It is too much like wanting the Jewish government to remain. The best thing would be to return East Jerusalem to Jordan. But the borders should be open. I should be able to go freely to parks in West Jerusalem.

I have been to Jordan only once. I would like to be able to visit other Arab countries—especially Saudi Arabia. There the Arabs are very wealthy and respected. The Saudis are putting up new gold on the Dome of the Rock here. When visiting Saudi Arabia, I would go on the *hajj*, of course, since the pilgrimage to Mecca is the most important thing a Moslem can do. But I would also bring back many good things to sell.

Nitza
(age 17)

Until I was eight years old, I lived on Kibbutz Ramat Rachel. I left with my mother and younger brother when my parents got divorced. I was real glad to leave kibbutz. I did not like kibbutz life. I am much too independent, and I like my privacy. Also, I did not have enough freedom on kibbutz. I was expected to do whatever the *metapelet* [caretaker] told me to do. I couldn't challenge her.

I was also happy to leave kibbutz because it meant that my parents would no longer be living together. All they ever did was argue. I never saw them show any affection to each other. In fact, they still argue all the time. Now they are bickering over the details of my brother's Bar Mitzvah. There's always something.

My father was born into an educated, successful family in Baghdad, the capital of Iraq. Before the War of Independence my grandparents lived in their own home with large grounds. Then, in 1948, there were anti-Jewish riots in Iraq, and all the Jews had to flee for their lives. My grandparents lost their jewelry business and their luxurious home. All they managed to bring with them were some Persian rugs and a little jewelry. When they came to Israel, they sold the jewelry. With the money they bought a motel in Haifa, a port city on the Mediterranean coast. They still have the carpets. They are now on the floor of my grandmother's home in Ramat Gan. My father's father has since passed away.

My mother's father was born in Jerusalem, and her mother in Poland. My grandfather is ninety-four years old. He has many stories to tell about all the wars in this country. He was a member of the underground Lechi fighters who helped Israel become independent from England. He was close friends with Menachem Begin and Yitzhak Shamir, who later became Israeli prime ministers.

A year after we left kibbutz my father also did. My parents now live a few blocks away from each other in Rehavia. They each have five-room apartments, and I spend time with both of them. But my father is almost always busy. He is a dermatologist. When he's not working at Sharei Tzedek Hospital, he is seeing patients in his private practice. He's busy from 8 A.M. to 8 P.M. My mother has more free time. She teaches Hebrew at Hebrew Union College.

My neighborhood is pleasant, but it is too quiet. There

aren't enough young people here. About half of the residents of Rehavia are older, retired people. My father is one of the few Sephardim around. The Sephardic Jews from places like Iraq or Morocco are more lively, more fun. There are too many German Jews in Rehavia.

I am happiest when I am in school. I am the kind of student teachers love. I like all my teachers, and I always want to learn. My favorite subject is literature. Perhaps that will be my major in college.

I also love to dance. For the past seven years I have been studying classical dance. I practice every day. Politics, too, plays a big part in my life. My number-one boyfriend is active in the Meretz movement. I campaigned for Meretz. And I've taken part in many demonstrations for peace. If only Meretz got six or more seats, they would have a bigger say in running the country.

I'd rather see Labor in power than Likud. But I think Rabin is weak. He should have thrown out the corrupt ministers in his cabinet, without worrying about the religious Knesset members in the coalition. And he needs to stand up more strongly to the settlers. The land on which they have settled does not belong to them. It belongs to the Palestinians. The settlers should be forced to leave it. The ultimate solution to any lasting peace is a Palestinian state. I think that the agreement with Arafat will help bring peace to the region. It is wise for Palestinians to support him instead of the Islamic fanatics.

I am optimistic that we can live together once the Palestinians feel more like equals. Areas like Gaza and Jericho should certainly be under their control. I am even ready to sacrifice the Golan for a chance at real peace with Syria. I participated in Meretz-sponsored rallies in favor of the peace agreement. I don't think that negotiating with a man like

Arafat means that we love him and approve of his actions.

I don't know any Arabs personally, but I would like to meet them. I have gone to meetings with religiously observant Jews. These meetings are sponsored by a group that tries to further understanding between religious and secular Israelis.

I have no problems with religious Jews who are part of Israeli life. But I don't understand the *haredim*. I don't understand any of their reasons for not serving in the army or doing national service. This exemption is not fair. I certainly pity the *haredi* women. They must be kept so weak to be controlled the way they are. I remember *haredim* in Mea Shearim shouting at my mother when I was young. All my mother did was walk by their neighborhood in a sleeveless dress.

I sometimes believe in God, but mostly in the God that is in all of us. I don't care for religious education, but after the Holocaust it is important for Jews to continue their culture and know something about their traditions. I would like to keep up observance of holidays like Passover, as my father does. My mother doesn't at all.

I have no interest in visiting Poland or Iraq, where my parents were born. Greece and China would be fun to see. I may get my chance after army service.

I am not looking forward to serving in the army. I don't want to leave my mother. I also think that the Israeli army discriminates against women. Women cannot rise to high ranks here. It isn't fair that women can't be pilots. During the Persian Gulf War I saw American women flying aircraft on CNN. I was amazed. Why can't girls be pilots here in Israel?

After the army I plan to study at Hebrew University. Then maybe I'll continue my studies in London. I have relatives there. It's my favorite place. Maybe I'll even decide to move there. Life in London is more civilized. I don't think I'd ever want to get married. My parents never seemed happy. But I would like to have a child someday.

I don't feel it's my responsibility to produce children for the state or for my people. I'm nobody's baby-making machine. Besides, with all the new immigrants, Israel has more people than she has room for. Crowded cities are no excuse for the Israeli government to allow some immigrants to live in the territories. You can't solve a problem with a new problem.

I feel sorry for all these new immigrants from Russia and Ethiopia. They came here with expectations for a better life. But there are not enough jobs for them. And the government is not doing enough for them. I just read that many of them are depressed. And I don't see where the jobs will come from.

But I am an optimist. As the Israelis always say, "It will be good."

Omer
(age 18)

It's a crappy country; what can I tell you? Until the army takes me away in three weeks, I'll still be living down in Baka with my parents. My mother's side is eighth-generation Jerusalemite, while my father's side came from Russia after World War I. My father is a professor of economics. He and Fidel Castro are the last freaking Commies left. My mother calls herself a freelance editor. In other words, she's looking for work like everybody else.

I went to the Givat Gonen school run by the Labor party. A lot of propaganda with some math and science thrown in. I don't want to be a Labor party leader. That's why I don't know what the hell I'll be doing for a living. Who cares? First let me survive my freaking three years of army duty. Why can't Israel have a volunteer army? Let them hire all the stupid bastards who want to play with guns. There are thousands of them. Do I need these goons with the officers' stripes playing with my head for the next three years? It's not the fast marches with full gear I'm talking about. It's all the psychological crap they pull on you.

What a laugh it was to see the *haredim* at the draft board. Not one of those creeps is going to see a day of service, but they are sweating bullets going through the paperwork. And they stink bad enough when they are not sweating. I say shoot them all! Why the hell are they allowed to vote in this freaking country? I can't imagine what is going on in their heads. I don't know what it must be like to believe in God.

This God thing certainly makes the Arabs crazy, too. What the hell do they want? A state? Give them Gaza, give them the West Bank, give them Greece for all I care. They won't be any security risk. We won't allow them to have an army. If they bring one little gun into this state, we'll overrun them in a second. Who gives a crap for their *intifada*? Nobody reads the papers about the latest strike or protest anymore. They have got to try behaving less like sons of bitches. This *intifada* crap got them nowhere.

I know what it's like to live in other places. We were in Canada for two years when my father was on a visiting professorship. I'll never make *yerida* and live with those cold bastards for the rest of my life. I don't know. Israelis are a special kind of race. The kids in other countries are such whimps compared to Israelis. Western kids can be real smart, but they are less mature.

I don't mind all the tourists asking directions in German, French, or English. But who wants all these new immigrants babbling away in Russian and Amharic? What kind of Israelis are these? They better to hell learn some Hebrew before they get in the army with me. I have nothing against black people or fish-face Slavics—it's just that I hate these suckers. Where is the next wave of immigrants going to come from? The Fiji Islands? Some anthropologist will prove that the Eskimos are a lost tribe of Israel and soon enough we'll have a million freaking igloos on Ben Yehuda mall!

I even get along better with Sephardim. Really: Almost half my friends are not Ashkenazim like me. The Sephardim are plenty of fun. They are only stupid when it comes to their right-wing politics. But I don't really have any Sephardic girl-friends. I'll let you know when I want to kiss a girl with a moustache. I may not get married at all. Who needs that crap? Besides, I hate kids.

What am I going to do to support other people? It's hard enough trying to get by as a single guy who lives at home. I've had some kibbutz jobs and I've tended bar. You can easily blow a few days' salary on movies and drinks. The economy sucks. But I'm not going anywhere. Not even out of Jerusalem. Tel Aviv is ugly. The kids are yuppies who look like crap. They are all so full of themselves. And for what? I hate the humidity there. I hate the ugly blocks of cement they live in. Forget it!

Here you look out the city bus and you see huge stretches on terraced hills on ten layers of history. If I survive the army and the hellhole in Lebanon that they throw me into, you'll find me right here. It's the only place.

Rafi
(age 20)

Congratulate me! I just got my visa today, and in three weeks I'll be leaving. For good! I've had enough of this country.

It is too hard to live here. Six months ago I finished a course in hairdressing. All I can make here—working in somebody else's salon—is about $400 a month. My friends in America tell me that they earn that in a week. And easily. Do you think I can afford an apartment on the salary I can earn here? An apartment in the worst slum on the outskirts of the city would cost me $350 a month.

So you tell me. How could I live? I only manage now because I live with my parents. We've lived in the same apartment in Neve Ya'akov for the past ten years. It's a pretty crummy place. All the criminals from the U.S.S.R. got dumped in my backyard. You'd think I was happy that a thousand blond girls moved into my development. But there are two thousand fathers and brothers watching them like hawks. Besides, I don't speak their language. The only language they want to hear is money.

Neve Ya'akov looks about fifty years older than it is. Lots of steps and terraces are falling apart. The cats love this place, though. Come hear our midnight concerts sometime. The Friday night music we hear is from *haredim* at their Shabbat tables. They seem to take lessons from the cats. Then we have our friendly Arabs next door. The number twenty-five bus to get here gets stoned half the time. That's why I drive. I take a different route. How can I afford a car? Okay, so I borrow my father's.

My parents? They are wonderful. They would never ask me to leave. But still I want my own place. I want to be independent. I don't like leaning on others. America will give me that chance.

This country is in for some hard times ahead. With Rabin in power I don't doubt that there will be a Palestinian state. The Palestinians took lessons from us. They are the Zionists these days. They have a dream, and they will not rest until it's fulfilled. In 1948 we settled for less than what we wanted, and in another five years they will, too. They will accept anything . . . as a stepping-stone.

You don't believe me? You just wait and see. It's inevitable. Name me one nation whose autonomy did not result in statehood. Besides, the Palestinians have the world's sympathy. If it were up to me, there wouldn't be any Arabs here in Israel. They have twenty-two states. We have one. And in our own state we are powerless.

Do you know how many times my car windows have been shattered? Once when I was on army service, I got out of my car and pointed my gun at three kids throwing rocks at me. Do you think they ran? Or even flinched? Do you know how powerless I felt? They knew I'd never use my gun.

Just this morning an Arab worker came in here. For a shave. Can you imagine me going to a barber in East Jerusalem? He'd slit my throat. They're free to go anywhere, and I have to arm myself just to walk around in my own country. So, tell me, who's oppressed here?

The economy . . . the politics . . . it all stinks. What's to keep me here? My parents left Morocco, not for a better life, but because they were Zionists. I'm leaving Israel for a better life. Wish me luck!

Re'em
(age 19)

This land is mine. But—for now—this country isn't. I was born nineteen years ago in Nazareth, but I am a Jerusalemite now. For the past two years I've been living in the dorms at Hebrew University on Mount Scopus.

Nazareth, my native town, is divided into three sections. In the valley live the Arabs, in Upper Nazareth are the new Jewish homes, and in between is the mixed section where I was raised.

Arabs and Jews live together in my neighborhood, though not on the same blocks. And, of course, any area where Jews are the majority has superior garbage collection, road maintenance, and water.

When I was younger, Nazareth was much more appealing than it is now. It was far less crowded, and everywhere there were open spaces. In the past ten years trees and meadows have been replaced by modern buildings. Loud and foul-smelling vehicles are everywhere. People drive by instead of greeting one another on the streets. And the people living in the new buildings often remain strangers to one another. When I was growing up, everyone knew each other. There is also a drug problem now in Nazareth. But because the suppliers and buyers are mostly Arab, the Jewish police overlook it.

Although Nazareth is rather peaceful, my home is a battlefield. I try to avoid going home as much as possible. My parents do not get along. My mother is tormented daily by my father. When he isn't beating her, he is yelling at her. He does not allow her any freedom. She wants very much to have a life of her own, away from the house and her four children. But my father feels that a woman's place is at home.

Money is not a problem. My father has worked for the past twenty-five years as a driver for Egged, the Israeli bus company. In fact, he met my mother when she was riding his bus to look for a job in Jerusalem. She was trying to land a job in the entertainment industry. She didn't get the job. She got married instead. But the price she pays for this marriage is too heavy. She survives now by ignoring my father as much as possible. My mother would love to get a divorce, but my father refuses to agree to it. He is too stubborn.

There is no way I will repeat my parents' marriage. My

boyfriend, a law student at Hebrew University, treats me as his equal. He loves me and lets me do what I want. I am more of a political radical than he is, but that hasn't been a problem. And we are both atheists. If my father were to find out that I have a boyfriend, he would kill me. Believe me. He would slash my neck. When my boyfriend and I are ready to get married, we will elope. I don't think my father will ever find out about him.

My boyfriend is half-Christian and half-Moslem, and my father could never accept that. My family is Christian, and my father goes to church every Sunday. He regards Moslems as primitive. Actually, my father wishes he were Jewish. He regards all Arabs as inferior to Jews. When I talk to him about a Palestinian state, he says he would rather live in a state run by Jews than one run by Arabs. He foolishly looks at the countries all around us, instead of the country that we Arabs here should become.

I cannot even begin to understand what can be going on inside my father's head. The Jews do not even belong in this country. It is not their land. By conquest the Jews drove my people out. They came here by strength of arms. And is it fair for the Jews to absorb thousands of foreigners from Russia and Ethiopia while denying the right of my people to return? If you will count the children and grandchildren of the Palestinians who had to run away in 1948, then we have millions more for our Palestinian nation.

Politically, we Palestinians have not acted with unified purpose. I, myself, support George Habash. He talks about returning my people to their entire land. Arafat is too much of a politician, too willing to compromise. He says he will settle for a state on the West Bank and Gaza as some kind of interim solution. But that is hardly fair. As far as Hamas goes, they are religious fanatics. They don't represent my values at all. They are quite dangerous and, sadly, they are gaining the upper hand among Arabs in Israel and in many other Arab states. It is too bad that the Iranian revolution was led by Khomeini instead of by a Marxist. Now the poor Arab looks to his religious leader for solutions instead of to the politicians. No matter which factions get initial control of the Palestinian people, we must continue the struggle to take back our land.

What right do the Jews have to any of this land? Even according to the Bible—which I do not believe in—the Canaanites, who were Arabs, were the original inhabitants of Palestine. Then Abraham fathered two sons, a Jew and an Arab. The Jew decided to leave and the Arab chose to stay. So whose land is this? Someone who leaves a land two thousand years ago cannot suddenly return and claim it as his. One hundred years ago, when the European Zionist Theodor Herzl had a vision of settling in Palestine, only 2 percent of the people here were Jewish. What about the other 98 percent? Were they invisible?

Sure the Zionists needed a homeland for the European Jews. I'm sorry about the Holocaust. I don't like seeing people die. But the Jews have killed too many of my people, and the Jewish Holocaust is not my problem. My problem is that of my brothers and sisters, the Palestinian refugees who escaped being slaughtered at Deir Yassin and dozens of other places.

There will be a Palestinian state. That is for sure. But it will take some time. In the meantime, I will do what I can to carve out for myself the best life possible here in Jerusalem. I am majoring in archeology with the hope of becoming a tour guide. Already, Christians I meet from all over the world are impressed that I am from Nazareth. I don't tell them that I think Jesus was much like me—a political radical.

To help pay my tuition, I have a part-time job working with autistic children. I am the only Arab where I work, and my relationships with my Jewish co-workers are cordial. I never discuss politics with them. It is impossible for even casual friendships to exist between Arabs and Jews once politics enters in the picture.

Even though I have the right to vote, I choose not to. And, of course, national service of any kind is out of the question. This puts me at a disadvantage. I do not have any of the benefits that the Jews who serve in the army have. I do not get any tuition breaks here at Hebrew University. And I do not live with honor. No Palestinian can live in a Jewish state and have self-respect. A few of my friends have chosen jail over the kind of life Palestinians are relegated to. One of them—accused of smuggling arms for Habash—died after being forced to sit on a glass bottle for hours on end. Most of my activist friends don't talk about their experiences in prison. It is forbidden to talk and, besides, life in prison destroys whatever is left of your body and soul.

I am committed to the struggle, but my work is with ideas instead of guns. After I am married, I wish to continue to live here in Jerusalem. Who wouldn't choose to live in Jerusalem? The people here are warm and the atmosphere is open. Intellectual and political activity is everywhere. I also love its discos and cinemas and nightlife. Sometimes when I walk alone, I worry about being stabbed by a Palestinian nationalist. I look Jewish, and I am often mistaken for a Jew. But that is a small price to pay for living in this special city.

Rivka
(age 16)

I have lived

here in the Rova, the Jewish Quarter of the Old City, all my life. So much has changed for us here—and all of the changes have been good. When I was a little girl, all this area was sealed-off ruins and a stoney parking lot. The Arabs had not rebuilt or settled into most of the Jewish homes and synagogues that they destroyed in 1948. All this beautiful plaza was built up in the last seven years.

These parks and smooth stone streets were not here when I was younger. It was not safe to play because of all the garbage and construction mess. Boys on donkeys would ride by and leave dirt wherever they pleased. Now you see all the cafés and restaurants here. All the Christian tourists who walk through the *shuk* and the Via Dolorosa come here to sit and eat. Here it doesn't stink of donkey urine and rotting fruit. We sweep and wash down our streets all the time. Everyone in the Rova knows that the eyes of the whole world are on us. And we are proud of this.

I don't know anyone whose parents were born here. I have met several Jews whose grandparents were born in the Old City. They don't live here now. They should be given special rights to return to their former homes. But this is difficult. We learned the history of the Old City and we know that Jews were the majority here for over a hundred years before 1948. I could see with my own eyes the holes in the doorposts where there used to be a *mezuzah*. Many more Jews should be living here, but what can we do?

My parents are both from France. Like Jews everywhere, they were very inspired by the Six-Day War. They had always been Zionists. They met at their B'nai Akiva youth group near Paris. When the war was over and all of the Holy City was in our hands, all the talk of one day moving to Eretz Yisrael got very serious. They moved here in 1971. They could not move in to the Old City right away because there was a lot of work going on with water pipes. My parents said that life was difficult here in the first few years. But they also said it was exciting. They were like pioneers.

It used to be that half the people in the Rova were artisans and people who sold antiques, postcards, or refreshments. Most of those people no longer live here. Some of them commute in from richer, safer neighborhoods. Those people in the Rova who work here now are in the Torah business. But I mean this with all due respect. Our greatest industry is Judaism and our biggest export is Jewish scholarship and good deeds. The *yeshivot* are our factories, and we are one of Israel's greatest "industrial zones." We are developing here different communities of Jews: Ashkenazim, Sephardim, Hasidim [followers of a sixteenth-century Eastern European Jewish movement]. And each has their own synagogues and *yeshivot*. We all expect the Rova to keep growing.

I went to school here until fifth grade. It was small and not well organized. Now I take the bus to an all-girls' *yeshiva* in the city. It is quite challenging and I like my teachers. I am not sure what I will do after I do national service. I have done volunteer work in day care centers, but I don't want to be a nursery school teacher. I wouldn't mind teaching in a high school. I have good friends, both girls and boys, in my B'nai Akiva youth group. I am not spending time with one particular boy yet. But, you know, I have my eye on someone I like.

I hope to be married and raising a family by the time I am twenty or so. I would like to live in the Judean hills in some brand-new settlement. We will be pioneers like my parents were here in the Rova. I want to help settle new lands and to claim them as our birthright.

If I miss the crowds and the excitement, I will come back to visit on the holidays. There is nothing like coming to the Kotel to see all the Israelis and tourists. I think I will be more spiritually moved if I only see the Temple area a few times a year. Now, I'm afraid, I take it all for granted. It is good for me to see outsiders coming to the Wall to cry their hearts out to God. They remind me that I am living an ordinary life in an extraordinary place.

Rochel
(age 16)

I am a ninth-generation Yeru-shalmi [Jerusalemite]. But I don't consider myself an Israeli. For eight generations my father's family has lived in Yerushalayim. And sixteen years ago I was born just a few blocks away from my current home.

I am part of the Jewish peo-ple, but not the Jewish state. Most of the people in my neighborhood don't vote, and no one serves in the army. The army kills your soul. We would leave this country rather than do army service. Before the Messiah comes, it is not possible to have a real Jewish state. We, the Jewish people, are still in exile.

I live in Geula. Our three-room stone house is on a narrow street near Mea Shearim. When I was younger, there were still some secular Jews on my street. Now there aren't any. Practically my entire neighborhood is *haredi*.

I would not want to live anywhere else. Living here, I never have to see the desecration of the Sabbath. Our streets are closed off to cars from Friday sundown to Saturday sundown. No one here plays a radio or television on Shabbos or any day of the week. You won't find *shmootz* [smut] plastered on walls or bus stops, and everyone dresses modestly.

People here are always involved in acts of kindness. Before my sister Rivka's wedding last year all the neighbors helped her sew clothes and then, after the wedding, they made *Sheva Brachos* for her [seven blessings, a week of festive meals for the married couple]. If some family member is sick, everyone in the community helps out. In my family there are seven children, but many families have as many as ten children.

God provides. We receive money from relatives who live abroad. They support our families and they support our yeshivas. My sister got married last year when she was seventeen. She now has a baby. When she was my age, the *shadchanim* [matchmakers] started calling our home to arrange a match. Before her engagement she met with her husband three times. Each time they spent two hours talking in the kitchen. Of course, the family was in the next room.

Her husband learns Torah most of the day, and conducts some part-time business. He sells holy books for an hour or two a day, just, you know, between *mincha* and *maariv* [the brief interim between afternoon and evening prayers]. I do not want my husband to have to work at all. I would like to marry someone who sits and learns from early morning until late at night. We will receive money from different sources. And if I have to work, I will.

I now teach first grade. I began teaching this year when I turned sixteen. I earn eight hundred shekels a month. We do handicrafts and teach the children *aleph beis* [the alphabet and reading]. We teach only in Yiddish, but the children need the Hebrew alphabet to read Yiddish, to read Torah, and to daven. All through school we study the Torah in Yiddish. *Loshin koidish* [the holy tongue of Hebrew] should only be used for Torah and davening. I do know some Hebrew. There are times when I have to speak it to buy something or answer a question.

My English I know from my mother. My mother was born in America. Her parents are good Jews, but they are modern and Zionists. My grandfather doesn't understand our way of life. It disturbs him that my mother speaks to us in Yiddish and that my brother has such long *payis*. But my mother feels that our way of life is pure, without the *treife* [unkosher, prohibited] influences that are part of the outside world.

My grandfather recently bought us our first radio. He said, "When Meshiach [the Messiah] comes, you will need a radio to hear the news." But here in Geula we don't listen to radios, watch TV, or read the newspapers. Even a radio carries women singing about immodest feelings. If there is any news that is for our ears, we will find out. People talk. Only during the Persian Gulf War did we get special permission from the rabbis to keep a radio on.

We all stayed calm during the war. Only the baby cried. We knew that our Father in Heaven would take care of us. We did put on our gas masks, but by the time we could get all the children's masks on, the siren sounded to remove them. Only my grandfather in America stayed posted to his radio day and night during the first few days of the war. He was worried that a missile would hit our home here in Geula.

We do not concern ourselves with the Arabs. We know that until the Meshiach arrives, we will not have peace with our Arab neighbors. The land of Israel does not yet belong to the Jews. It does not belong to the Arabs either. My rebbe teaches us that the Holocaust was a punishment for all the Zionist activity. My father tells us that the Zionists prevented many Jews from being rescued in the Holocaust. They didn't want thousands of religious Jews coming here to ruin their socialist paradise.

Before 1948 my father's mother lived in the Old City. She had many Arab neighbors. They were like family to her. They shared their vegetable crops and goats' milk. But on the day that Ben-Gurion declared a state, her dearest Arab friend stood on her rooftop and yelled, "Kill the Jews." She will never forget that.

The *goyim* will never accept the Jews until Meshiach's time. But we shouldn't make them angry by trying to rush. The Hebron massacre of *yeshiva* students only happened after the godless Zionists began fighting for a state.

I wish that everybody lived the way we do. When every Jew keeps Shabbos, the Messiah will come. Until then we have to be concerned with HaShem's [the Name, God] punishments for breaking the Torah. The *intifada* began when the Jews began to open movie theaters in Jerusalem on Shabbos. If not for this state, many more Jews would be religious.

I do not like to leave my neighborhood. It hurts to walk on Jaffa Street and see *freyer* [nonreligious]. I hope someday that they, too, will be part of the Jewish people.

Sa'ana
(age 14)

I am from

Ramallah, just north of Jerusalem. My parents before me were also born there. My two sets of grandparents had lived in Irbid and Aljun, towns in what was then called Transjordan. They moved to find work, just as my father travels in to Oorshalem [Jerusalem] six days a week to paint houses.

During summer vacation my father sometimes brings us here to Liberty Bell Park while he is working in the city. Two years ago my father bought a large Volvo automobile. We now can get to Oorshalem in a quarter hour, with no waiting for the blue bus to Jaffa Gate. Last summer we didn't come once to Oorshalem. The situation was not good. Things are much better now.

There are three girls and two boys in our family. I am the middle girl. My older sister no longer travels with us. She stays home because she is in her engagement year. Today we had special treats in our picnic to celebrate our grape harvest. We all worked very hard to cut grapes in our fields. We also grow vegetables, but not for market. They are only for ourselves and for trading with neighbors.

I go to a religious girls' school in Ramallah. I'm best in the sciences. I don't think about having a career after school. Such is not our way. I will be married when I finish school to someone my father has negotiated with. I would like to make my home over here in East Jerusalem. Abu Tor is where I would most like to live. I have some family there, too.

The trouble is worse in Ramallah when things are bad. My oldest brother is in jail now for four years. The authorities say he was involved in killing collaborators. If this is true, then I can't say my brother did the wrong thing. What can you do about your own people who inform the authorities on your activities?

Last year we had a bad incident with the Border Patrol. The Druze soldiers came in and threw our dinner all over the place. They also broke our kitchen table. This was the only time they came into our house. Outside the house my grandfather received a wound in his arm from a rubber bullet. He was not doing anything wrong. He was only in the way of soldiers who were shooting at demonstrators. Things are quiet now, but the police still want 350 shekels for some tax my father refuses to pay.

When there is a strike called by the PLO, my father does not go to work and we do not go to school. We are all strongly behind Arafat. He lived through Lebanon, he lived through a plane crash, he lived through the Likud period. *Inshallah*—he will be president of an independent Palestinian state. We want nothing to do with King Hussein. What did he do for us? Words are cheap. When there was a brief *intifada* in Jordan, he slaughtered us.

My parents did not vote in the elections. We are not Israeli citizens. Besides, there was nothing for us to vote for. Things may go more quickly now for a political settlement. But no one danced when Rabin came into the government. The only party we watched was the party that called for our transfer. Now it looks like there is nothing to be concerned about.

No one in my family was hurt in the wars. When Saddam's missiles were flying in the Persian Gulf War, we took no safety measures. We were prepared to die along with our enemies. The war did nothing for us. But we were happy at the time because there was hope that things could change.

Whatever happens, I don't want to live anywhere else. If I could, I would visit Saudi Arabia and the United States. My parents have gone to Saudi Arabia on the *hajj*. I expect to go to Mecca as a pilgrim at least once in my life, as the Koran commands. I don't have to move anywhere to be in a Palestinian state where there is dignity and peace. Such a state will come to us.

Sami
(age 18)

Look into my eyes! I don't hate Jews at all. I don't care about politics. I only want a better life.

I was born in the Arab neighborhood of Wadi el Joz, a valley just north of the Old City. My father came to Jerusalem from Jordan about forty years ago. My mother was born here in Palestine, in the town of Nablus.

The school I attended was in the Old City. I learned some Hebrew,

English, and French there, but all the teaching was done in Arabic. My best subject was recess. I love soccer and I'm very good at it. I'm in a league that plays teams from other neighborhoods.

It would be a dream to play soccer for money. Instead, you will find me in the Machane Yehuda marketplace hauling boxes of vegetables from 7 A.M. to 8 P.M. four days a week. I don't earn more than six hundred shekels a month. I also don't get much respect. For my bosses I am a donkey with two legs. I have done some house painting, too. This is much better because your work is set out for you. There are no four bosses telling you what to bring all at the same time.

I tried to work at a Jewish hotel where my cousin works. They told me they are only hiring Russians. To really work on my own, I must get a tractor-trailer license. I did some driving with my father's friend, but I got arrested because I didn't have the license. I would like best to work in America. I would be able to go if only I had family there. Many people I know would move to America if they could. The work here is difficult and the wages are low. At least now there are fewer strikes and almost no trouble with the government. Many people I know were hurt in the *intifada*. My mother was hurt trying to get my brother away from an army truck. The truck was taking boys away for detention after a demonstration.

It is not the Israeli army that is cruel. It is the Border Patrol made up of Druze and Beduin Arabs. They hate us and treat us like dung. They come into our homes and break furniture. We have to hide our women. We complain to the police, but they do nothing. The Border Patrol arrested me for no reason. They were more cruel after Rabin told them to break our bones. We did not forget this. In my family we voted for Likud against Rabin.

The Druze would like to keep it going, but I think the

intifada is over for good. I don't want an independent state and I don't want to be with Jordan. After the Russian immigrants it is clear that there will be no state of Palestine here. And East Jerusalem will not be connected to any Palestinian area in the territories. There are Jewish neighborhoods all around us.

I have an Israeli identification card. But it does say Arab on it. We get health benefits and stipends for each child in our family of eleven. My family needs more money and more room to live. I don't have enough money to marry the girl of my choice. My older sister's and brother's marriages were arranged. We are all religious Moslems. God is the one who made the sun and the waters. That is why I pray five times a day.

Shai
(age 19)

Sure I'm the age for army duty. I'm finished with it. Really, they are finished with me. I spent eight months in an army prison. It was hell. Hey, it wasn't my fault. The army wouldn't let me see my mother when she was sick. She had a heart attack. Her fifth one. In fact, the army was sending me far away to Lebanon. That's why I ran away. I had to be with my mother then. And sure enough she died when I was in the stinking prison. Then the bastards let me out.

There was nobody else at home. My father didn't count. He and my mother were divorced. Look, I'm going to tell you the whole story. I don't tell many people. You're going to cry. Believe me.

My parents were born deaf-mutes. They put people like that together. They had nothing in common. Mama was from Syria. She had a kind heart like you wouldn't believe. She would give you her new shoes if you needed them. Not my father. He's from Poland. He wouldn't give you his old shoes.

I have four older brothers. Do you think they stick around to help? They are all in Canada trying to make a successful business. I'm the baby. I stay here and have to put up with my father. It's his damn apartment I'm living in. But I don't get a sheqel from my father. I wouldn't take one from him. I work painting houses. But, you know, it's hard to find more than one or two jobs in a month.

Sure I went to school. I stayed until the eleventh grade. A year or two more than most of my friends. But here's the part that will break you up. Things got bad with my parents when I was about ten. My father let religious people come and take me away to a *haredi* boarding school in Tel Aviv. They were Belz Hasidim. I tell you I was kidnapped. I wore black and had my hair shaved down except for long *payot*. At first it was better than what was going on at home. Then it got too much for me and I ran away.

I got into trouble. My parents weren't together then, so the social workers put me into a *haredi* foster family. It was horrible. I can't even talk about it. For over a year now I'm back home. My father says bad things to me in sign language. I've made up a few signs to tell him things back.

I like it better here downtown than in my neighborhood. Here I get free pizza and Coke from American writers asking me stupid questions. Hey, I'm only kidding. I'll tell you what I don't like about Romema. It's near the central bus station, so a lot of people like us live over stores. Then, there are too many cowboys around. That's what we call the *haredim* because of their big hats. If I'm on the corner with my shirt off, they look at me like I'm an animal. Some of them have the nerve to tell me how to dress. And they have the *chutzpah* to say that they also work for the country—by praying and learning. They are swaying back and forth like a dog in heat while the rest of us are risking our lives.

I'm not against religion in general. I believe in God. It's just bad that prayers don't get answered. I learned this the hard way. I go to synagogue on Yom Kippur. If everyone believed in God, I think the Messiah would come. Right now there is still too much hatred in people's eyes.

I can't afford to get married too soon. Maybe when I'm twenty-four. Believe me, I have no lack of girlfriends. I have the look. Just like Luke Perry on "90201." I could marry and live out of the country. A quiet, dull country might be nice— maybe Holland.

Yankle
(age 17)

I do for a living what my father does. We sit and learn the holy books. Our life is devotion to Torah study and performance of the *mitzvahs*. This is a real living. Working in the physical world is an unfortunate thing that takes one away from holiness.

My grandfather knew what such work meant. He was sent to a forced labor camp in Siberia by the Russians. Many didn't survive the terrible cold, the backbreaking work, and the poor conditions. Still, we are thankful to the Holy One Blessed Be He that he survived and brought my father here as a young child. My mother also came here as a baby. Her family survived the Holocaust by hiding from the Nazis and fleeing to Romania. There were many losses from both sides of the family.

My parents are both from Satmar Hasidic families, and their marriage was arranged for them when they were sixteen, just like it was for me. I have only one brother and one sister. Only HaShem knows why the family is so small. Most of my relatives have, *Baruch HaShem* [blessed be God], ten or more children. I only have one baby at home, but I've only been married for a year. I don't worry about how to support many children. Everything is possible with the help of God.

I grew up in the Kiryat Sanz neighborhood of Jerusalem. I started religious school at about age two and a half. There is nothing holier than the sounds of the little children singing out verses of Bible and Yiddish translation. You can hear their chirping everywhere in Mea Shearim, the neighborhood I moved to after my pre-rabbinic yeshiva.

I have never wasted time on secular learning. After reading and writing, the only thing we learned besides Torah was counting and figuring. This isn't mathematics. I understand that students spend time learning figuring exercises that they can never use in business or life. This is surely a waste of time. There are no government rules telling us what to learn.

After going to the same yeshiva as my father in Kiryat Sanz, I decided I wanted to learn here in the Brestlover *kollel* [where married men learn intensively]. This was a different path from my father, but it is not, God forbid, any kind of rebellion. I was attracted by the teaching of Rabbi Nachman of Brestlov and was influenced by some friends who also came to this *kollel*.

If you look at my sidelocks and black jacket, you might think I'm a Hasid. I don't consider myself a Hasid. Hasidism is more concerned with serving God with open joy and public deeds, while the Brestlov path is more quiet, removed from the physical world. Our task is trying to increase the world's level of holiness. Of course, we have a *rebbe*, too, but Rav Nachman of Brestlov died a few hundred years ago.

There are ways that we get close to our *rebbe*. Many of us take the path of meditation and prayer. We all try to visit Rav Nachman's grave. I went last year, and will try to go at least once a year now that I'm married. Some of us go three times a year. A group of three thousand of us traveled to the Ukraine to be at the grave at Rosh Hashanah [Jewish New Year] time. This is a special time and place to have prayers answered.

This trip is my greatest expense of the year. It cost about seven hundred dollars. But Rebbe Nachman requests it, and this precious opportunity is worth the price of three or four months of food. I also make a few trips to the graves of our great saints and martyrs here in the Holy Land, in places like Safed and Tiberias. Other than these I do not travel. I do not wish to see other places or live outside of Jerusalem. These trips take me to other times and energies, not other places.

Next year I will have to get a note from my *kollel* to exempt me from the Israeli army. I will have to do this once a year until age forty-five. It would be like death to be taken by the army. It is impossible to be God-fearing in such circumstances. The army is full of deniers of God, people engaged in Sabbath desecration and sexual impropriety. It is not my place to talk of such things as politics, but there should not have to be an army. The troubles that come from Ishmael [biblical term for the Arab nation] and Esau [term for the Christian West] could be solved in spiritual ways.

The more important battles are not for land or peace. They are for holiness. There is a hatred here for holiness by the forces of the Other Side, the powers of the Satan. I see hatred in the eyes of the God-deniers. They look at us like we are donkeys. Secular culture is the Hitler of our time. This satanic force wants to destroy the Jewish souls of Russians, Ethiopians, and the new Yemenites who come here. The deniers are not concerned with freedom of choice, only the spiritual destruction of Torah Jews. I have friends who fought with police over public Sabbath desecration on the roads. The deniers don't understand the pain that their behavior causes.

The first time I ever thought about marriage was when my father came to tell me that he had a girl for me to meet. I prayed about meeting my intended one. The two families met, and I had some time to speak to her in another room. She was also sixteen. She had fine qualities of modesty and dedication to Torah. The match was made. She was the only potential bride I met. This is the way I prayed it should be.

Then came all the arrangements for the wedding and the new apartment. The night of the wedding my father told me about a husband's duties, that is, how to perform the commandment of "be fruitful and multiply." This was very shocking for me. I could not believe it, so I asked my rabbi. He said the same thing. I had read about certain laws of "using the bed," but I couldn't imagine being engaged in something so, so very physical. Such are the mysteries of God's ways. I am only sorry that I wasn't married at fourteen.

I have spoken too much already. I don't want to be photographed, and I don't make a habit of talking to strangers.

All work, all contact with the state and the outside, material world are to be limited as much as possible. Holiness, only holiness, is to be increased.

Yehezkel
(age 19)

I was six when my parents made *aliyah* from St. Louis to the Land of Israel. Both sets of grandparents are still in America. My father's parents don't talk to us at all. They are upset that my father became religious and moved to the Land. We didn't move here to the Old City right away. We first lived in the Kiryat Moshe section. That's where I attended a religious public school before coming here to Ateret Cohanim *yeshiva* in the Moslem Quarter. I walk to yeshiva from our home in the Rova five minutes away.

My father had been a lawyer, but is now doing some computer programming. More important than anything professional, my father and I are rebuilders. He is involved in restoring the Jewish community of Hebron and expanding their museum. I give a lot of my time to recovering the Jewish presence here in the Moslem Quarter. It shouldn't even be called the Moslem Quarter. There was a higher percentage of Jews living here than in the Jewish Quarter during the mandate. The British made up these names. They don't mean anything.

You see the hollow cut in the doorway of this building? There was a *mezuzah* here. A Jewish family built this house and lived here for hundreds of years. You'll see many such doorways in this part of the Moslem Quarter. Often the entire stone is taken out so the evidence isn't so obvious. The Arabs are not the legal owners of most of the homes here. They became squatters after the murderous riots of 1926 and 1939 cleared away most of the Jewish residents.

Once again Arab aggression was rewarded. This time it wasn't the usual Jew-haters in the U.N. or State Department, but the fearful Israeli leftists. The Arab squatters here became protected tenants under the foolish Israeli law, but the deeds of ownership are still held by Jews. Even the Jordanian records say this.

Don't believe anything you read about Jews throwing out Arabs from their homes. Every time Jews move into the Moslem Quarter, there was a long, legal, and expensive story behind it. I know. I have helped my *yeshiva* through the long process. It begins with a set of Arab middlemen who tell us that a certain home is willing to be sold to us for a huge price. The original Jewish owner is researched, and a release from his heirs must be obtained. Everything has to be done very quietly and indirectly since both Jordan and the PLO have pledged to kill anyone who sells a home to Jews. Even the corpse and spirit of such a home seller is banned from a Moslem cemetery and damned for eternity. So, you see, everything has to be done through seven veils.

The seller has to be set up with a new identity, a new country, a new job, and a new home. All this work by our contacts in Switzerland or the U.K. costs hundreds of thousands of dollars. The seller gets met at the airport and driven to his new life. And all because his grandparents squatted in a Jewish home and obtained tenants' rights. How we get them false passports is a different story. I can't talk more because Ateret Cohanim is in enough trouble with the Rabin government over some financial help we got in the last several years. The media reports are all wrong. Most of our reclamation money comes in from donations overseas, not from the government and certainly not from the families who move in. The people who move in are usually large religious families with limited means. These people are eager to get along with their Arab neighbors and want only to live close to the Temple Mount.

The biggest stink has been raised over the so-called Church of the Sepulchre building. You know that big mess in the media about Jews breaking into a church during Easter? Don't believe a word of it. The building involved wasn't part of the church. The big hall there, in fact, was used for Jewish weddings in the thirties. It recently became an unoccupied security area of the Israeli army after a drug bust. Some Christian Arabs were just upset that they didn't get the empty building, so they went to their friends in the media. There was moving of people and furniture before and after Easter, but all those Jewish Jew-haters in the media reported it on Easter. That's when the networks are all over the place covering the Christian pilgrims in the Christian Quarter.

Sometimes it is true that an Arab appears to be beaten up when Jews are moving in. To protect themselves, some agents for sellers demand that they get beaten in public, in broad daylight, and with at least one camera crew rolling. They have to make it look like they were forcibly evicted. They especially like to be taken away by ambulance so their Arab neighbors don't kill them or their families. The martyr game is worth a few bruises for them.

And I think these Arab sellers are smart as well as brave. They are getting big sums of money from us and getting out of a place where there is no future for them. Have you seen the way most of them live here in this quarter? They have one or two small rooms for ten people and no modern conveniences. When I asked where the plumbing was in one house we were looking at, they showed me a pail with a rope.

Under Jordan the Arabs had no sewer system, no electricity, no universities. But I can't blame them for not saluting the Israeli flag. Many Arab homes in the Baka, Talbieh, and Katamon areas of Jerusalem ended up on our side of the Green Line. I wish them only good things. I hope they can be happy and prosperous in places that need them. They should rebuild and settle in Arab areas depopulated by wars. There are many such areas in Lebanon, and civil wars will open up more of Iraq and Jordan.

Never mind East Jerusalem. There's no future for Arabs in all of Judea and Samaria. Ever since the *intifada* the Arabs have been boycotting Israeli products. They are no longer good for the economy. When most construction and blue-collar jobs are filled by Russian and Ethiopian immigrants, Arab emigration will pick up.

This is a miraculous time, despite all the setbacks. There

are religious problems with the Jewishness of the Ethiopians. There were many intermarriages over two thousand years, so a conversion ceremony for new brides and grooms should be standard. Of course, the Russians are quite intermarried, too, but we have the records from seventy years ago. Many of the ones that stay are going to be good Jews and important Israelis.

Along with the Arab Knesset seats, it was the Russians who put Labor in power. The majority of veteran Israelis did vote for Likud. Labor was smart to hide their leftist policies and just emphasize Yitzhak Rabin. The Russians and many others were more concerned with paychecks than with the sanctity of Jewish land.

I don't think it's impossible that a civil war could break out over Rabin giving away parts of Eretz Yisrael. I, myself, could never shoot at an Israeli soldier. If I were on a newly "illegal" settlement that was attacked by Arabs, I would certainly fight back. There is too much weakness in the army now. A soldier has to consult with his lawyer before lifting his gun to defend against Molotov cocktails.

I have a *yeshiva* exemption from the army right now. But this is only a deferment of two years. I just didn't want to interrupt my studies in the middle, but I wouldn't think of trying to avoid army service altogether. That would be a desecration of God's name. The *haredim* are still in the eighteenth century. They don't know that to have a beard, *payis*, and *tzitzit* [ritual fringes] with an army uniform is a sanctification of God's name.

Despite the few murders of *yeshiva* students in the last ten years, I don't feel any danger when I walk around here in the Moslem Quarter. There was more fear in New York City when I visited there two summers ago. Here I have a permit to carry this pistol. You didn't see it because I always wear my shirt over the holster. I don't want the provocation of a visible weapon. My smile is a better defense. There are many Arabs who call out my name when I pass by. I tell you that most of them are happy that Jews have moved in. They know the place will be kept cleaner and safer.

I can show you buildings where a mosque and a rabbi are living under the same roof. The Arabs who recognize that HaShem or Allah has reserved this tiny land for the children of Israel can stay here in peace. As for the crazy radicals who ignore the Koran and the Torah, who needs to talk to them? If they got all of Israel, they'd start fighting to reconquer Spain.

I don't believe the Labor party can make peace. Only HaShem can make peace. We gave everything to Egypt and nothing to Jordan. So why is Jordan the quieter border? All we need to offer our neighbors is peace for peace.

Yehuda
(age 16)

I've been in Israel now for four years. My parents decided to move here so that we could live a Jewish life. I had spent the first twelve years of my life in Greenwich Village, New York—not exactly the best place for an Orthodox Jew. I still remember the whiffs of marijuana drifting into our apartment overlooking Washington Square Park as my father made *kiddush*. And as I'd walk the streets of the Village wearing a *kipa*, I'd get comments like, "So what are you planning to be . . . a doctor, or a lawyer?"

In fact, I plan to be neither. I would like to eventually run my own construction company. I know I have to start small. Do the kinds of work that the Arabs do. But eventually, with hard work and solid planning, I will make it to the top. And that's no thanks to the business atmosphere here. You gotta fight the tight network of government-protected companies if you're gonna beat 'em with some American-style free enterprise.

My biggest gripe with this country is its educational system. It's not education. It's indoctrination. And it does nothing to prepare you for the more competitive society that I want to live in. I might switch to a vocational *yeshiva*. Carpentry is the only thing I enjoy in my present school. I only left shop because the crazy Moroccan kids were too much for me.

I might even drop out of school in the tenth grade and just study to pass the *bagrut*. If I don't pass, it won't be the end of the world. I'm not into learning a lot of things that aren't useful. My parents still value Western culture too much, and even had us take French lessons for a while. It's probably because they became religious later in life.

I'm not sorry we moved here, but Israel is not the ideal place for a teenager from America. I never really feel accepted by the Israeli kids. In my *yeshiva* in Hebron they just tolerate me. They have no choice. But I don't feel there's any real bond between the Israeli kids and the American ones. What we do have in common is that we all get arrested. We've all been picked up by the Israeli police at one time or another for · assaulting Arabs. To me, though, it's not assault. It's defense. If an Arab kid my age is throwing stones at me, what am I supposed to do? Naturally, I fight back. I've been picked up and released a number of times for beating up Arabs. It's part of life in Hebron, which is in the heart of Judea-Samaria.

I don't just pick up rocks and throw back. I run after them. I'm not afraid. Soon I'll be old enough to be allowed to carry a gun. I'm all for minority rights, but nobody has the right to express themselves with rocks and knives. Hebron is full of reminders of Arab violence against innocent Jews. We have a memorial here with photos of Jews who were axed and stabbed all over their bodies. Every time I come here to learn, I keep alive the memory of the *yeshiva* students who were slaughtered in the 1930s. Hebron must be reclaimed as a Jewish city because the Arabs trashed the synagogues and Jewish community here.

Right near my *yeshiva*, I should say "a stone's throw away," is the burial cave of the biblical ancestors of the Jewish people. Anyway, the Arabs put a building up over the tombs, and there's a lot of tension about Jews and Arabs sharing the same holy place for prayer. Abraham is holy to Arabs, too, since he's the father of Ishmael—the first Arab. In fact, this is when all the problems started. Ishmael was Abraham's first son, but he was from Abraham's second wife, Hagar. She was an Egyptian woman who served Sarah. Sarah had Ishmael and Hagar thrown out when Ishmael was threatening her son Isaac.

I'm not a political person. But if we ever had to give up any of this land in biblical Judea, I'd probably end up in jail. I'd fight to keep what is rightfully ours. In another two years I'll be in the army. That's okay. I can use the discipline. I'll take what I can get out of that experience. There's something to learn from everything.

When I'm not in *yeshiva*, I live with my family—my parents, my fourteen-year-old brother, and my three younger sisters—in Kiryat Wolfson. These are some of the highest apartment buildings in Jerusalem. You can see Sacher Park and the Knesset from my window. It's a nice neighborhood but there aren't enough kids. A lot of apartments are left empty, especially in the winter. You hear English about half the time, so it's not much of a real Israeli neighborhood.

I could see myself spending time in other countries besides Israel. But I would want the main home I raise my family in to be a place like Kiryat Arba, near Hebron. It's got a nice mix of 60 percent religious and 40 percent secular. I don't want a religious ghetto, and I don't want a secular Tel Aviv either—where everyone wishes they were in L.A. The secular Jews in Kiryat Arba are respectful. They don't ride cars on Shabbat. I wouldn't mind if my kids played with these kinds of secular Jews.

Real improvement will only happen when the best parts about America are brought in, like an open economy and direct elections. Of course, the trashy American things, like the stress on image, don't belong here in a Jewish country. Israel is not yet a Jewish country, but it's the only one we've got.

Zadiya
age 14

I was born

in the Israeli half of Beit Sefafa. There are two halves of my village. In 1948, following Israel's War of Independence, our village was divided into two parts. Half of the people who live here are citizens of Jordan and half are Israeli citizens. Since the war of 1967 both halves are under Israel's control. But the split remains. Our friends and relatives who live in Jordan can visit us freely. But Jordan will not allow those of us with Israeli passports to cross the [Allenby] bridge into Jordan. Those in the other half of our village are much more in touch with their families in Jordan. Both my parents and grandparents were born in this same village. I have one younger brother and one older sister.

Hamas does not speak for me or my family. Although we believe in Allah, we are not Moslem extremists. Only Grandmother prays every day. And she only prays in the morning. We support Yasir Arafat and the PLO. The *intifada* has helped us get to this stage of talking about our own state.

When we have a Palestinian state and when Israel returns our land to us, there will be peace. This land belonged to us for two thousand years. Israelis and Palestinians will be able to live with one another once there are two separate states. If the future Palestinian state does not include my village, I will stay right here. I do not ever want to leave Beit Sefafa.

My father works for the municipality of Beit Sefafa. He is the head gardener. He employs both Arabs and Jews. My father has special status because he is a professional soccer player. My mother works as a secretary in an architectural firm. Her office is in East Jerusalem, just outside the walls of the Old City. Everyone who works there is Arab.

Both my parents voted for Meretz in the last election. I don't know if it really matters who is in power. I, myself, have both Arab and Jewish friends. I recently attended an Israeli camp with young people from both East and West Jerusalem. Just yesterday I visited a Jewish friend in nearby Kiryat Yovel.

I will be beginning ninth grade next month in our local school. I attend school six days a week, from 8 A.M. to 2 P.M. My favorite subject is Hebrew; my least favorite is Arabic. I began studying Hebrew in the third grade. I love speaking and reading Hebrew. I recently read a book in Hebrew about the *Shoah*. I hadn't yet learned about it in school.

During my free time, when I'm not roller skating or playing basketball, you can usually find me at home watching television. My favorite television show is "Zorro." I also love watching American movies. With a television nearby, I am never bored or lonely.

The girls in my village do not date. Sometimes we see boys secretly. Most of us marry by the age of twenty. Although our parents choose our partner, we have a say in the matter. If I'm lucky, I will get to marry someone I really like. I will let my friends know which boy appeals to me. Once both of our parents know what we want, they will arrange the match.

Once I am married, I plan to raise my family right here in Beit Sefafa. With the help of God and Arafat there will be peace.

PROFILES OF INTERVIEWEES

NAME	AGE	M/F	BACKGROUND/NEIGHBOORHOOD
Abed	19	M	Moslem Palestinian/Silwan Village
Alon	15	M	Israeli/German Colony
Ani	20	F	Armenian Orthodox/Armenian Quarter
Ariella	12	F	American-Israeli/German Colony
Avner	18	M	Israeli/Beit HaKerem
Chaim	13	M	American-Israeli/Pisgat Ze'ev
Dalia	17	F	Australian-Israeli/Kibbutz Ramat Rachel
Dan	18	M	Ethiopian-Israeli/Katamon
Daniella	12	F	Israeli/Talpiot
David	12	M	American-Israeli Baptist/Bethlehem Road
Dawoud	18	M	Christian Palestinian/Wadi el Joz
Efrata	17	F	Israeli/East Talpiot
Ephraim	13	M	Israeli/Pisgat Ze'ev
Gina	15	M	Baku-Israeli/Pisgat Ze'ev
Leah	14	F	American-Israeli/Har Nof
Leonid	14	M	Russian-Israeli/Neve Ya'akov
Liat	15	F	Israeli/Pisgat Ze'ev
Limor	17	F	Israeli/Kiryat Yovel
Louis	15	M	Christian Palestinian/Christian Quarter
Mark	14	M	Dagestani-Israeli/Baka
Muhammad	14	M	Moslem Palestinian/Abu Tor
Nitza	16	F	Israeli/Rehavia
Omer	18	M	Israeli/Baka
Rafi	20	M	Israeli/Neve Ya'akov
Re'em	20	F	Christian Palestinian/Mount Scopus
Rivka	16	F	French-Israeli/Jewish Quarter
Rochel	16	F	Haredi Israeli/Geula
Sa'ana	14	F	Moslem Palestinian/Ramallah
Sami	18	M	Moslem Palestinian/Wadi el Joz
Shai	19	M	Israeli/Romema
Yankle	17	M	Hasidic Israeli/Mea Shearim
Yehezkel	19	M	Israeli/Jewish Quarter
Yehudah	16	M	American-Israeli/Kiryat Wolfson
Zadiya	14	F	Moslem Palestinian/Beit Sefafa

JERUSALEM MILESTONES

1900 B. C. – 922 B.C.

While ancient Egyptian and Assyrian records refer to the city as early as four thousand years ago (1900 B.C.), the Israelite king David conquered Jerusalem from the Jebusites about 1000 B.C.—or three thousand years ago—and made this inland, mountainous city the new capital of the Israelite kingdom. Also called the City of David, Jerusalem reached its peak of regional glory and power under David's son, King Solomon, who built a magnificent Temple to the Lord. A remarkable period of peace reigned supreme until Solomon's death in 922 B.C.

63 B.C. – A.D. 33

Jerusalem's population reached some two hundred thousand by the time the new super-power, the Roman Empire, captured the city in 63 B.C. It was under Roman rule that the great Christian drama of Jesus' life and death was played out, largely in the streets of Jerusalem. It was here that Jesus of Nazareth, a Jewish rabbi (teacher) reputed to have powers of healing, had to be wary of ruthless Roman over-lords, their corrupt secular Jewish allies, and the defensive religious minority.

A.D. 70 – 132

After four years of revolt against the Roman Empire, the Second Temple and the city of Jerusalem were destroyed in the year A.D. 70. The Romans rebuilt the city and renamed it Aelia Capitolina, making it a capital of their province of Palestine and a center for pagan worship. In the year 132 the Bar Kokba revolt gave the Jews three short years of inde-pendence, the last they would have for nearly two thousand years.

922 B.C. – 438 B.C.

The northern tribes broke off to become Israel, while the south, called Judea, remained centered in Jerusalem. The mighty Babylonian Empire defeated and exiled the ten tribes of Israel, destroyed Jerusalem in 587 B.C. and took many surviving Judeans captive. When the Persian Empire (modern-day Iran) replaced the Babylonians as the regional power, the emperor Cyrus allowed Ezra and Nehemiah to lead several thousand Jews back to Jerusalem. By 438 B.C. Jerusalem was again the center of Jewish culture.

322 B.C. – 64 B.C.

In 322 B.C. the Greek Empire under Alexander the Great conquered the entire Mediterranean area. In 167 B.C. Syrian-Greek king Antiochus IV raided Jerusalem's Second Temple and tried to force the Judeans to adopt paganism. Led by the Maccabees, the Jews fought a successful three-year guerrilla war which is celebrated in the festival of Hanukkah. Jerusalem was rededicated and independent once again. The Jewish Hasmonean kingdom emerged after 168 years of Seleucid and Ptolemaic (Greek) dominance.

A.D. 132 – 614

As the Roman Empire adopted Christianity as the state religion, few Jews were allowed to live in or visit Jerusalem for several centuries. The Byzantine Empire (Christian) replaced the Romans. Inspired by his mother's pilgrimage to Jerusalem, Emperor Constantine (288–337) built shrines including the Church of the Resurrection. In 614 Jews conspired with Persian invaders and, for a few months, began preparing the city for a Third Temple. The Byzantine Empire fought off the Persians, however, and kept the area's Jews on a shorter leash.

The Seventh Century A.D.

In the seventh century the Middle East was engulfed by a new power. The faith of Islam, founded by the prophet Muhammad, had united the tribes of Arabia and set out to conquer the region in a jihad, or holy war, for Allah (God). In 638 the Arabs took control of Jerusalem. The caliph Omar remodeled an octagonal Byzantine church into a magnificent domed mosque (Moslem house of worship) that stands over the original Temple Mount. Called the Dome of the Rock, its golden dome makes it a major Jerusalem landmark.

A.D. 638 – 1077

While the pagans of the Near East and North Africa were forcibly converted, the Moslems tolerated Christians and Jews as "people of the book," as those following older prophets like Moses and Jesus. With the belief that Muhammad ascended to heaven from the Dome of the Rock above the Temple Mount, Jerusalem became Islam's third holiest city after Mecca and Medina in Saudi Arabia. Called *Al-Quds* (the Holy) in Arabic, Jerusalem was a spiritual center for all three monotheistic faiths but was not used as a secular capital city for any Christian or Moslem republic.

A.D. 1077

The Seljuk Turks (a Moslem but not an Arab people) conquered Jerusualem in 1077. Twenty-two years later the Crusaders from Europe took the city, displaying Christianity's undying claim on the Holy City. The bloody attack for the glory of medieval Christendom brought Arabs, Jews, and Turks together to fight side by side.

A.D. 1537 – 1917

For hundreds of years Jerusalem remained a small walled city, significant only as a spiritual address for prayers and occasional pilgrimages. West Jerusalem, the Jewish neighborhoods outside of the Old City's walls, first got settled at the time of the American Civil War. When Turkish rule ended, after Lawrence of Arabia helped the British defeat the declining Ottoman Empire, Jerusalem had 47,000 Jews, 16,400 Christians, and 9,800 Moslem Arabs. The city only began a major population boom under British rule, 1917–1948.

A.D. 1917 – 1948

Under the British mandate many thousands of Jews streamed into Palestine (the British reviving this old Latin name) from Europe, while many Arabs did likewise from surrounding countries. There were bloody struggles between Arabs and Jews, even though both wanted the British out. After World War II the British did leave, planning to divide Palestine into Arab and Jewish states. Jerusalem was to have been an international city. Not ready to accept such terms, the Arab nations of Egypt, Syria, Jordan, Lebanon, and Iraq attacked the newly declared state of Israel in 1948.

A.D. 1187 – 1517

The Turks retook Jerusalem in 1187, and the returning Crusaders replaced crescents with crosses from 1229 to 1244. By the time the Mongols swept past and the Mamluks took over, Jerusalem would be a poor and sparsely populated city for the next few centuries, from 1250 to 1517.

A.D. 1517 – 1537

Order and new life came to the city after the Ottoman Empire's (Turkish Moslems) takeover in 1517. Many of the new immigrants were Sephardic Jews fleeing the Spanish expulsion in 1492 and the brutal Inquisition of forced Catholic converts that followed. In 1537 the Turkish sultan Suleiman the Magnificent rebuilt the city, including the thick stone walls and gates that still circle the Old City today.

A .D. 1948 – 1967

The Israelis won the war and their first independent state since Second Temple days, but they lost the Old City of Jerusalem to the Jordanians. The Jews of the Old City were expelled, and their synagogues and cemeteries destroyed. Many Arabs were uprooted from southern neighborhoods, joining the hundreds of thousands of Arabs made homeless in the Arab-Israeli wars. The second of these wars to involve Jerusalem was in 1967, when the Israelis captured the Old City. The barbed wire walls separating Arab and Jewish Jerusalem were torn down, and all faiths were given access to their holy places.

A.D. 1967 – present

Jerusalem has mushroomed into Israel's largest city. The 1993 population of 564,300 included 73% Jews, 24% Moslems and 3% Christians. (The Holy City was toured by 94,000 Christian pilgrims in 1987.) Historic agreements with the Palestinians, the Vatican, and Jordan took place in 1994, but Jerusalem still remains the focus of controversy. If the three great faiths of the Western world can truly walk together in peace, it should be past the stones of ancient, modern Jerusalem.

GLOSSARY

aleph beis (also known as aleph bet)—the Hebrew alphabet and reading skills (literally: "the first two letters")

aliyah—(Hebrew) immigration to Israel (literally: "ascent")

Allah—(Arabic) the Almighty, the monotheistic deity of Islam

Amharic—language spoken by the Ethiopians in Ethiopia. Many of the older Ethiopian immigrants continue to speak it at home in Israel.

Anglo-Saxim—(Hebrew slang) immigrants from English-speaking countries

Ashkenazim—(Hebrew) Jews of central and Eastern European descent

bagrut—(Hebrew) national exams for high school graduates

Baruch HaShem—(Hebrew) thank God (literally: "Blessed be the Name")

bet knesset—(Hebrew) synagogue (literally: "house of assembly")

Bibi—Benjamin Netanyahu, the Likud party's opposition leader

chutzpah—(Hebrew) nerve; guts

daven—(Yiddish) pray

derech eretz—(Hebrew) good manners (literally: "the way of the land")

Eretz Yisrael—(Hebrew) the land of Israel

fez—(Arabic) a felt cap often worn with a tassel

GLOSSARY

freyer—(Yiddish) nonreligious Jews (literally: "free")

frum—(Yiddish) religious Jews

galut—(Hebrew) exile; life outside of Israel

Gemorah—(Aramaic) the Talmud, 1st century set of legal and biblical studies

goy (goyim, pl.)—(Hebrew) non-Jew (literally: "nation")

hajj—(Arabic) Moslem pilgrimage to holy sites in Saudi Arabia

Hamas—(Arabic acronym) fundamentalist Moslem group that wants the entire Middle East under Koranic rule

haredim—(Hebrew) ultra-Orthodox Jews (literally: "fearful ones")

HaShem—(Hebrew) God (literally: "the Name")

Hasidim—(Hebrew) followers of sixteenth-century Eastern European Jewish movements stressing piety and wearing the distinctive clothes of their dynastic groups

hesder yeshiva—(Hebrew) school that combines learning of Jewish texts and military service

Hizballah—(Arabic) pro-Iranian Party of God based in Lebanon

imam—(Arabic) Moslem religious leader and teacher

inshallah—(Arabic) with the help of Allah (God)

intifada—(Arabic) uprising against ruling authorities (literally: "shaking off")

jihad—(Arabic) Holy War to widen the spiritual and physical domain of Islam

Kach—(Hebrew) ultra-right-wing political party whose founder, Meir Kahane, was raised and assassinated in New York City

Katyusha—(Russian) portable rockets, fired by Hizballah fighters against Israeli settlements in the north

kibbutz (kibbutzim, pl.)—(Hebrew) a collective farming settlement

kibbutznik—(Hebrew) one who lives on kibbutz

kiddush—(Hebrew) ceremony over wine to sanctify holiday

kipa—(Hebrew) skullcap worn by observant Jews

Knesset—(Hebrew) Israeli parliament

kollel—(Hebrew) school of Jewish learning for married men

Kotel—(Hebrew) the Western Wall, sacred remnant of the Holy Temple's outer wall

limudei kodesh—(Hebrew) religious subjects

loshin koidish—(Yiddish/Hebrew) the Hebrew language (literally: "the sacred tongue")

makolet—(Hebrew) grocery store

Masorati—(Hebrew) traditional; in Israel the Conservative movement is referred to as Masorati.

Meretz—(Hebrew acronym) left-wing Israeli party

Meshiach or Moshiach—(Hebrew) the Messiah (literally: "the one anointed"—as King of Israel)

mezuzah—(Hebrew) small covered scroll of biblical texts traditionally placed on doorposts of Jewish homes and buildings

midot—(Hebrew) good characteristics

mitzvahs or mitzvoth—(Hebrew) commandments

Moledet—(Hebrew) right-wing Israeli party that advocates the "transfer" of Arabs (literally: "birthplace")

mosque—(Arabic) Moslem house of worship

oleh (olim, pl.)—(Hebrew) immigrants to Israel

Oorshalem—(Arabic) Jerusalem

payis or payot—(Hebrew) sidelocks (worn by ultra-Orthodox Jewish males)

protectzia—(Hebrew) influential contacts

rebbe—(Yiddish) rabbi and communal leader, especially of Hasidic sects

Rosh Hashanah—(Hebrew) the Jewish New Year

Rova—(Hebrew) quarter; Jewish Quarter of the Old City of Jerusalem

sabras—(Hebrew) native-born Israelis (named for native fruit that is prickly on the outside and sweet on the inside) *seichel*—(Hebrew) sense or intelligence

Sephardim—(Hebrew) Jews from northern Africa and Asia with roots in Sepharad, or medieval Spain

Shabbat or Shabbos—(Hebrew) the Sabbath; Saturday

shadchan (shadchanim, pl.)—(Yiddish) matchmaker

Shas—(Hebrew acronym) Sephardi religious party

Shechem—(Hebrew) biblical term for Arabic town of Nablus

Sheva Berachot or *brachos*—(Hebrew) a week of festive meals for a newly married couple (literally: "seven blessings")

shmootz—(Hebrew, Yiddish) smut; dirt

Shoah—(Hebrew) the Holocaust, organized extermination of millions of European Jews during World War II

shuk or *souk*—(Aramaic, Arabic) marketplace

Taimani—(Hebrew) Jew from Taiman or Yemen

tallit—(Hebrew) prayer shawl worn by observant Jewish men at prayer

tefillin—(Hebrew) ritual prayer straps of leather holding boxes containing scrolls of biblical texts

Torah—(Hebrew) the Hebrew bible or extended religious texts

ulpan—(Hebrew) language institute where Hebrew is taught

yerida—(Hebrew) emigrating from Israel (literally: "descent")

Yerushalayim—(Hebrew) Jerusalem

Yerushalmi—(Hebrew) Jerusalemite

yeshiva (yeshivot or yeshivas, pl.)—(Hebrew) school where Jewish texts are studied intensively

yored (yordim, pl.)—(Hebrew) emigrant; one who leaves Israel

Zhid—(Russian, Slavic) derogatory name for a Jew

■ BIBLIOGRAPHY ■

Abodaher, David J. *Youth in the Middle East: Voices of Despair.* New York: Watts, 1990.

Anderson, Bob, and Janelle Rohr, eds. *Israel: Opposing Viewpoints.* New York: Greenhaven, 1988.

Clayton-Felt, Josh. *To Be Seventeen in Israel: Through the Eyes of an American Teenager.* New York: Watts, 1987.

Collins, Larry, and Dominique Lapierre. *O Jerusalem!* New York: Pocket Books, 1980.

Elon, Amos. *Jerusalem: City of Mirrors.* Boston: Little Brown, 1989.

Goldston, Robert. *Next Year in Jerusalem.* Boston: Little Brown, 1978.

Gorkin, Michael. *Days of Honey, Days of Onion.* Boston: Beacon, 1981.

Indinopulos, Thomas A. *Jerusalem Blessed, Jerusalem Cursed: Jews, Christians and Muslims in the Holy City from David's Time to Our Own.* Chicago: Ivan R. Dee, 1981.

Rosenwasser, Penny. *Voices from a Promised Land: Palestinian and Israeli Peace Activists Speak Their Hearts.* East Haven, Conn.: Curbstone Press, 1992.

Said, Edward W. *After the Last Sky: Palestinian Lives.* New York: Pantheon, 1986.

Shipler, David K. *Arab and Jew: Wounded Spirits in a Promised Land.* New York: Times Books, 1986.

Sichrovsky, Peter. *Abraham's Children: Israel's Young Generation.* New York: Pantheon, 1991.

Wallach, John, and Janet Wallach. *Still Small Voices.* New York: Harcourt, 1989.

Wiesel, Elie. *A Beggar in Jerusalem.* New York: Random House, 1970.

ACKNOWLEDGEMENTS

We are grateful to the young people of Jerusalem who shared pieces of their day and their lives with us. Another teenager, Sara Ching Mozeson, was often there to put our interview subjects at ease and to be our recording engineer.

We were most fortunate to work with publishing professionals on the caliber of our literary agent, Mary Jack Wald, and our editor at Four Winds Press and Simon & Schuster, Virginia Duncan. Her staff of Andrea, Christy and Michael is both creative and personable.

Our talented photographer, Leora Cheshin, became a good friend over the many hours of photo safaris she led through the hills and valleys of Jerusalem's widely varying neighborhoods.

Of the Israeli and Palestinian contacts who made the book possible we are most grateful to our generous friends Hanita Roz, Sylvia Z. Cassuto, Suri Granek of Pisgat Ze'ev,and to our enthusiastic Arabic translator, Abed Misri of Silwan.